THE ASSASSIN'S HEART

The Assassin's Heart

CHUCK MORGAN

THE
ASSASSIN'S HEART
A ROMANTIC THRILLER

BY

CHUCK MORGAN

COPYRIGHT © 2025 BY CHUCK MORGAN

Printed in the United States of America
First printing 2025
ISBN 979-8-9923558-6-4 (Paperback)
LIBRARY OF CONGRESS CONTROL NUMBER 2025902482

DEDICATION

To the readers who seek thrills, love and the courage to defy expectations. May this story ignite your imagination and remind you of the power of a single heart to change the world.

INTRODUCTION

Delia Cahill lived a double life. By day, she was a hardcharging attorney to some of the richest people in the world. She was a loving wife to her unassuming government employee husband. She wrote contracts for huge amounts of money and got her clients out of unpleasant situations when they'd broken the law, but she also baked cookies, watered her roses and volunteered at the local animal shelter. She was all things to all people.

But as the sun dipped below the horizon, her transformation began. The gentle, almost ethereal Delia vanished, replaced by a woman of deadly skill, a worldclass assassin.

Her life was a balancing act between two worlds that should never collide. But fate, as it often does, had a way of disrupting the planned order of things. Delia's latest assignment, to eliminate a tech billionaire who had created an app capable of tracking the nuclear submarine forces of every nation, presented a challenge unlike any she had ever faced. This was no ordinary target; he was a man shrouded in mystery, a recluse who held the power to ignite global chaos.

However, as Delia moved closer to her objective, she was drawn to the billionaire, his enigmatic presence unraveling the walls she had built around her heart. His vulnerability, his hidden pain resonated within her, challenging the very core of her being.

Delia, trapped between her duty to her shadowy employer and her burgeoning respect for a man who could potentially destroy the world, faced an agonizing dilemma.

Would she follow the path she had known for so long, or risk everything to protect the man who had awakened a longing she hadn't felt before? This choice would test her skills, loyalty and the essence of her soul.

Prepare yourself for a journey into a world where shadows dance, secrets whisper and love becomes the ultimate weapon. Delia Cahill's story is about to unfold.

CONTENTS

| 1 |

Death in Paradise

Robert Masters looked over the balcony rail of his penthouse apartment atop the Royal Hawaiian Resort and thought about how lucky he was. The sun was setting over the Pacific Ocean, and there was a light breeze off the sea. He looked behind him at his three sons horsing around in the living room. He smiled. Ever since his divorce from their mother, he had been too busy to spend a lot of time with the boys—ages seven, nine and thirteen—and he was excited that their mother agreed that he could bring them to Maui for two weeks of fun in the sun.

Robert was fit for his fifty-three years, muscular, with a full head of blond hair and bright blue eyes. He looked like he could still surf with the best of them, which was how he'd spent his early years as a professional surfer. Robert was listed on every charity auction as one of Los Angeles's most eligible bachelors. Of course, it didn't hurt that Robert also ran one of the largest investment and hedge fund companies in the country.

Masters and Cooper Capital, Inc., had more than 300 billion dollars in assets and had a client portfolio filled with notable entertainers, athletes and politicians. The people who knew him best knew him as a man of high integrity and honesty, and after thirty years, he still had almost all of his original clients, a fact that didn't go unnoticed when soliciting business. By every measure, Robert Masters was an American success story.

Robert had hoped that the seven-hour flight in his private jet would have knocked out his sons, but as he watched them clowning around, he had a huge smile on his face. He stepped into the living room.

"Okay, guys. Let's get dressed nice and we'll go grab some dinner. I know just the place."

As the boys headed towards their rooms, Robert picked up the phone, dialed the concierge and asked the woman who answered to make a reservation for four at the Cove Restaurant, one of the best and most popular seafood restaurants on the islands. Since the owner of the Cove was one of his clients, he knew there would be no issue getting a table.

Dinner was a success, as the chef/owner, Michael Sinclair, had a variety of dishes brought to the table. The boys were in heaven, and Robert spent a lot of time taking pictures with his phone and sending them to their mother. As the night wore on, he noticed the boys tiring, and he called for his car to be brought around. As they left the restaurant, Robert didn't notice the beautiful woman sitting at the bar watching him.

The following morning, the boys were up early, and after a breakfast fit for a king, they put on their swimsuits and headed to the beach at the back of the resort. The first thing you needed to do if you wanted to enjoy the islands was to learn how to surf, and he had rented four surfboards. He was excited to teach his sons something that he loved so much. He wished he could get away more and spend a little time on the water, but he always seemed to be too busy. This was his chance to enjoy a couple of weeks of surfing and get the boys into something that they could share back in California. They slipped into their swimsuits and headed for the beach behind the resort.

The beach was crowded with sunbaked tourists, but Robert found a spot away from the swimmers where the waves looked to be breaking nicely against the shore. He didn't want to push the boys too hard on their first outing.

They set down their blankets and a cooler that had been packed by the resort with lunch, snacks and drinks and grabbed the surfboards. Robert spent most of the day working with the boys on their surfing technique, and as the sun set into the Pacific, he felt happy for the first time in a long time. The day had been perfect. Only one thing would make it more perfect: one last big wave. He scanned the horizon and spotted the bigger waves breaking a couple of hundred yards offshore.

"Boys," he said, "warm up. I'm going to grab one more wave." He pointed towards the larger breakers. "See those big waves out there?" The boys nodded.

"You keep watching, and I'll show you how your old man used to surf when I was a kid."

The boys were excited as their dad grabbed the board and ran into the breakers rolling up on the shore. He surfaced and paddled hard for the big breakers, nosing under several smaller waves. He reached his launch point and looked back. He would need to be careful. There were a lot of swimmers in the area, but he would not miss out. He sat up on his board and looked towards the horizon.

He watched as the first set of waves rolled under his board, but he was waiting for the larger set that was forming. He lay on the board and watched over his shoulder as the first wave in the set approached. He was getting ready to paddle when his board flipped and he went under the water.

As the bubbles cleared, he felt an arm wrap around his chest and then a sharp pain under his ribs, and the surrounding water turned crimson. He struggled to breathe but kept swallowing water, and the arm held him under. As his life drained away from him, his last thoughts were of his boys.

The third wave of the set passed, and the surfboard with Robert lying on it broke the surface. His sons, watching from the beach, were waving and calling his name, but he didn't respond. They watched as several more wave sets passed under the board, but their father never moved.

Robert Junior, the oldest, ran towards the lifeguard stations and, after a lot of pointing and gasping for air, returned to his brothers followed by a tall, thin lifeguard. The lifeguard walked to the edge of the water and watched the board and surfer bob gently on the swells.

Wrapping the strap from his lifesaving buoy around his shoulder, he dove into the waves and swam towards the surfer. As he approached, he noticed what looked like blood pooling on the surfboard and washing into the sea. He moved closer and tapped the surfer's limp arm hanging off the board. There was no response. Getting behind the board, he kicked, held on and let the waves push the board towards shore. As he reached the shore, three more lifeguards ran into the surf and captured the board. They carried it onto the beach and laid it next to where the boys' blankets were lying on the sand.

A crowd had gathered and stood silently, many taking pictures with their phones. One lifeguard rolled the surfer off the board onto the blankets, and that's when they noticed a wound in the surfer's chest. There was a gasp from the crowd. They checked for a pulse but didn't find one. One of the other lifeguards pulled out a phone and called the police.

| 2 |

Silent Predator

The Cove Restaurant hummed, a low thrum of conversation and clinking glasses reflecting off the polished mahogany bar top. Delia Cahill, perched on a stool, swirled her chilled white wine, its citrus scent a faint counterpoint to the salt tang clinging to the sea breeze drifting in from the open windows.

Her reflection—a vision in shimmering sequins and five-inch heels—also showed four men, dismissed with barely a glance, already retreating into the crowd. Each rejection was a silent flick of the wrist, a subtle shift of her long blond hair cascading over her shoulders. The dress, a daring slash of fabric, clung to curves that were the stuff of legends, leaving little to the imagination. Men watched, some openly, others stealing glances from behind newspapers. Even the women, Delia noted with a wry smile, seemed to adjust their posture, their attention drifting towards their companions with a new intensity. A leg crossed, a thigh glimpsed—a deliberate move that sent a ripple of awareness through the room.

Her skin, bronzed to the sheen of polished amber, seemed to absorb and reflect the warm island light. She was a goddess, casually holding court. The heavy oak door swung inward. Robert Masters, a man carved from granite and seasoned by years, entered, followed by three young men, his sons. Chef Michael Sinclair, the owner, a man whose girth hinted at both generosity and years spent mastering the culinary arts, greeted them with warm bear hugs—not crushing, but long enough to communicate deep respect and affection.

He seated them at a window table overlooking the moonlit ocean. The parade of food began: plates piled high with succulent seafood, vibrant salads glistening with olive oil, a symphony of colors and aromas.

Delia watched, picking listlessly at her shrimp salad, the wine a cool comfort in her hand. The dossier—a neatly typed list of the man's past and present—flashed in her mind: Masters was the financial angel who'd launched Sinclair's career with a helping hand and a hefty investment. The chef's gratitude radiated from the kitchen like heat.

As the evening progressed, the sons' laughter faded into quiet exhaustion. Delia waited, a subtle shift in her posture signaling her readiness. But the opportunity never presented itself. Masters and his sons, surrounded by the satisfied murmurs of fellow diners praising the exquisite food, disappeared into the night.

Delia finished her wine, the last drops clinging to the glass like a whispered promise. She signed the bill, leaving a generous tip that brought a broad, grateful smile to the bartender's face before she glided out into the night, leaving a trail of allure in her wake.

Delia was enjoying a quiet breakfast at the poolside lounge when she spotted Masters and his son heading towards the beach. They stopped at a small shack, entered and left five minutes later, each carrying a surfboard, carefully chosen for their sizes. She tracked them as they headed for the farthest end of the beach near the large rock outcropping, just at the edge of where the sun-loving tourists were setting out their blankets and coolers for some time in the sun.

She finished her breakfast, made a trip to her room for a quick change and, now armed with her blanket and several bottles of water, headed for the beach. She found a spot near the family, laid out her blanket and slipped off her robe. Even though the bikini she wore accented her incredible curves, she felt it was modest enough for her purposes, covering more of her than she saw on other women. Still, men stared.

She covered her eyes with her sunglasses and lay on the blanket. She casually watched as Masters taught his sons the fine art of surfing. His dossier had mentioned that in his youth he was a world-ranked surfer, and she could see from his muscles that he still took care of himself, although his pale skin showed he spent a lot of time indoors. The dossier also included information regarding his comfort with certain members of the white supremacist movement and his involvement financially in several plans to overthrow the government of the United States. Delia was never told who the client was, but she could assume that it was some government agency.

As the sun slipped into the sea, she heard Masters tell his sons he was going to take one more wave before they retired for the evening. He grabbed his board and dove into the surf, paddling past the breakers.

Delia slipped off her sunglasses and pulled a pair of swimming goggles from her bag and put them on. Looking around, she carefully slid the razor-sharp composite knife from its sheath in the bag and, holding it next to her thigh, walked into the water and dove under the waves. She surfaced several times, each time closing on her target, like a shark circling its prey. She watched him lie on the board and glance over his shoulder at the approaching wave set.

She dove and surfaced behind the board out of his line of vision. He looked forward, and Delia dove under and flipped the surfboard. Masters fell off the board and slipped underwater. Delia came up from behind, wrapped her arm around his neck and shoved the blade deep into his chest. The blade pierced his skin like a hot knife through butter. The water turned crimson around them. Masters struggled, his mouth gurgling, his eyes large and his screams silent, and she held him under. She felt the fight leave his body as he gasped for his last breath.

Delia surfaced for a quick breath and dove again. She pulled the surfboard close to her, and with the board in front of her, hiding her from the beach, she tipped the board and slid Masters's lifeless body onto it. The surfboard bobbed on the incoming swells. Delia dove and made her way back to the crowds of swimmers and walked up onto the beach as she saw Masters's oldest son running towards her along the beach, followed by a lifeguard. His other sons were waving and yelling for their father to respond.

Delia reached her towel, removed her goggles and put them and the knife back into her bag. She put on her sunglasses and, like the surrounding crowd, stood and watched the unfolding drama as more lifeguards ran to the area to await the surfboard now being pushed ashore by the first lifeguard. Delia picked up her bag and walked towards her room. Sirens could be heard in the distance.

Twenty minutes later, Delia was in her rental car on the way to Kapalua Airport and the private jet, fueled and sitting on the tarmac, ready to take off as soon as she arrived. She sent her boss a text, letting him know she was on her way home after a successful conference.

| 3 |

The Revelation

Delia had gotten home late. The flight from Maui landed at the Burbank Airport at 2 A.M. She walked to the parking lot, slipped into her SUV and headed home. She knew David, her husband, would be asleep, so she pulled into the garage, parked and stepped into the house. She dropped her suitcase next to the washing machine and headed to her bedroom.

She stripped off her clothes and slid under the covers, waking David with a gentle touch and her body pushing against his. He never seemed to mind being awakened that way, and he responded with all the passion she had been hoping for. It was a ritual for Delia, but it worked after completing an assignment, and since David never minded, she was fine with it. After some passionate lovemaking, they fell asleep in each other's arms.

Delia woke to the smell of coffee and bacon cooking. She threw on a robe and walked down the stairs to the kitchen. David stood at the stove turning the scrambled eggs, and he looked over his shoulder and smiled.

"Morning, beautiful," he said. "Good client meeting?"

Delia poured herself a cup of coffee, set it on the table and walked behind him. She undid the belt on her robe and pushed her body against his back. She reached around, and her hand rested on his zipper, and she could feel him respond. He pushed her hand away.

"Eggs are ready, and I have an early meeting that I can't be late for."

Delia stepped back and laughed while tying the belt on her robe. They sat at the table and ate.

"Hey, don't forget I have that thing after work tonight," said David, standing and putting his plate in the sink. "Shouldn't be too late."

"No problem," said Delia. "I was planning on going to the office. I'll call you if I'm gonna be late."

She stood and followed him to the front door. He picked up his backpack and turned to face her. Delia pulled open the top of her robe, exposing her breasts, grabbed him, pulled him close and drove her tongue deep into his mouth. He responded in kind and then reached up and twisted one of her hard nipples. She giggled like a schoolgirl, and they both laughed as they stepped apart.

"Hold that thought till later," said David.

Delia closed her robe and laughed. "Sorry, big boy. You had your chance. I may just have to go find someone younger and more willing to bend to my wild ways."

David pulled the door shut, and Delia walked back to the kitchen to finish her coffee. She pulled her phone out of the pocket of her robe and flipped to her news feed. The story stopped her cold. The story about the death of Robert Masters while on vacation in Maui was the lead headline.

Delia never followed up on her assignments, but what caught her attention was the first couple of lines detailing all of Masters's charitable contributions and his philanthropic works. The number of hospital wings and pediatric cancer centers he had created in low-income areas struck her.

She should have stopped reading and moved on, but something compelled her to continue. By the time she got to the end of the article, she wondered what the hell she had done.

Delia poured herself another cup of coffee and headed for her small home office. She opened her desktop, and for the next several hours, she ran a thorough background check on Robert Masters. When she finished, she sat back. There was nothing in his background that suggested any interactions with white supremacists, not even speculation. From everything she could discover, using digital sources that reached deep into the halls of our government, Robert Masters was a kind, warm-hearted, caring man who spent a fortune each year taking care of those less fortunate.

Delia was pissed. She had spent her life putting bad guys and scumbags in the ground, but she had never knowingly killed anyone who didn't deserve to die.

Delia pulled out her phone, sent a meeting request and then headed for her room. She showered, dressed in jeans and a T-shirt, grabbed the holstered pistol from the hidden compartment in her closet and headed for her SUV. She needed answers.

When she arrived at her destination she parked her SUV and slid out. She pushed open the door and walked to the table in the center of the room. The director stood as she walked up to the table, and he could tell after all these years that Delia was more than pissed. He waved off the two guys who moved towards him from the corners as Delia scowled.

"Delia, I know why you're here. Since the story broke this morning, I have gotten several calls, all asking the same question. All I can do is give you the same answer as I gave them," he said. "We were unaware."

"What the fuck do you mean, unaware?" she asked, her voice echoing through the open space. "We killed a man who was a fucking saint. Who fucked up?"

"We're looking into that," said the director as he sat and placed his hands on the table.

"Who was our client?" asked Delia.

The director hesitated. "The client came through another agency. We made a mistake. We assumed the information had been vetted. Now that other agency is scrambling to figure out who gave us the bad intel."

Delia leaned on the table and stared at the director. "I want a fucking name."

"You know I can't do that. If word got out."

Delia slammed her fist on the table, and everyone jumped. "If word gets out we killed an innocent man and left three young boys fatherless, our reputation won't be worth shit. Now, you get on the phone and work your magic and you find out who wanted this man dead. I will take care of the rest."

The fire in Delia's eyes made the director uncomfortable, and Delia noticed in her peripheral vision the two guys reach under their jackets. She stood up and looked from one to the other.

"If you want to go home tonight, you had better pray that you're faster than I am."

The director looked at the two men and shook his head. They slowly pulled their hands from under their jackets and stepped back farther, like they were trying to avoid the line of fire.

Delia looked back at the director. "We violated a sacred code. We kill bad people; we do not kill people without a damn good reason, and this time we had no reason. Get me the fucking name of the person who set up this hit."

The director knew better than to argue at this point. He knew Delia had a code she lived by, as did all his people, and the Organization had just violated that code. He sat back and nodded. Delia stood and turned towards the door.

"I will get you a name, but before you leave," said the director, "I have another assignment for you." Delia turned and walked back to the table.

| 4 |

Shadowy Intentions

The old warehouse was a nondescript brick building surrounded by a sea of nondescript brick buildings. Anyone looking closely would have seen years of neglect and failure, many of the old signs still portraying the hopes and dreams of business owners now long forgotten. The old building was a perfect spot for a clandestine meeting.

The room was sparsely furnished, a single flickering fluorescent bulb casting long, grotesque shadows across the concrete floor. Two chairs sat separated by a small wooden table. Delia sat opposite the director, his eyes not looking directly at her. He had a reputation for ruthlessness, a reputation he had built with the blood and sacrifices of others. He had a strong sense of right and wrong, and he used that to make sure that those who did wrong were punished.

Delia Cahill was five foot ten, blond and beautiful, with an athletic body men would drool over. Trained as a lawyer, she had graduated at the top of her class and passed the California bar exam on the first try. Her life would have been perfect, except it was all a lie, a deep cover created by the Organization. She needed to be available at a moment's notice, so her backstory said she gave up corporate law and started her own practice with a handful of extremely wealthy clients, spread out all over the world. Clients she needed to visit occasionally. Her marriage to David was the only real thing in her life, except that all the guests who had attended the wedding on her side were coworkers with deep backstories as well.

"The target is a liability," he said, his voice a low, gravelly whisper. "His creation, that app, is a weapon waiting to be unleashed. It could tip the balance of power, leaving the world on the precipice of chaos. We cannot allow that to happen."

His words were devoid of emotion, the cold logic of a man who saw the world in shades of gray. Delia knew this. She had dedicated her life to the Organization, to their clandestine agenda, to their vision of a world sculpted in the shadows. The price of that commitment was a life lived in the margins, a double life shrouded in deception and danger.

"What are his vulnerabilities?" she asked, her voice a quiet murmur. Her eyes, however, burned with a cold intensity, the reflection of a thousand targets, a thousand lives extinguished.

"He's a recluse, a technocrat obsessed with his creation. He is isolated, vulnerable to manipulation." The director paused, his eyes cutting through the gloom. "Find his weakness, exploit it. Eliminate him and bring us the programming for the app. We cannot let this fall into our enemy's hands."

The assignment was simple, the execution a brutal celebration of death. Delia was a shadow flitting through the darkness, leaving whispers of her passage. She had honed her skills over years of training, becoming a weapon of unmatched precision. There was an art to it, a cold, efficiency. The thrill of the hunt, the intoxicating rush of power. It was all she had ever known.

Alexander Thorne had cracked the code of global communication, creating an app that could penetrate any system, any network, any defense. It was a tool of unimaginable power, a weapon that could cripple nations, destabilize governments and ignite global warfare.

She had seen the reports, the images of Thorne. He was a tall, enigmatic man with jade-green eyes and a quiet intensity. He seemed to radiate an aura of power, his gaze unsettlingly profound. There was something about him that set him apart from the other targets, a complexity that intrigued her.

The director, sensing her hesitation, spoke again. "We have vetted this target. I know you're pissed about the last assignment, but don't let your emotions cloud your judgment, Delia. This is the world's fate hanging in the balance. You are our last line of defense against chaos. You are our weapon. Execute the mission, and our future as a planet will be secure. We have one week to execute this contract. After that, Thorne has threatened to release this app as an open source, which will give all the enemies of good a seat at the table. There is a lot of money, billions, trying to get him to change his mind and sell to the highest bidder. Neither one of those is the answer we want."

"Why not buy the app, if it's that important?" asked Delia.

"We could, but there's a lot of powerful countries and entities interested, and we would have no guarantee that he would accept our bid. To be honest, some agencies of the U.S. have had some difficulties in dealing with Mr. Thorne. He is an erratic wild card, and we can't take that chance. Several U.S. agencies have been negotiating with him for weeks, but he is unwilling to make a commitment to them. They're running scared. We also do not know if he will abide by the terms of a sale and not release it to others anyway. He doesn't need the money, but with that kind of power, who knows how he'll respond?"

His words were like a cold slap to the face, a reminder of her place in this shadowy world. She knew better than to question the reason for a hit. She hadn't in the past, and she felt he was giving her more information than she needed because he knew how pissed she was over Masters. She was a cog in the machine, a weapon to be used. She was an instrument, a silent assassin, but she was also a human being, a soul capable of feeling, capable of doubt.

She would follow the protocol, complete the mission. The assignment was clear, the target identified. The world hung in the balance, and Delia would do her job.

| 5 |

The Target's Profile

Delia stood at the window, her reflection a stark contrast to the moonlit cityscape sprawling beneath her. Her face, a canvas of flawless perfection, was marred by the faintest hint of fatigue, a testament to the long hours she'd spent studying the dossier of the man who was about to become her target.

Alexander Thorne was a tech titan whose app, named Nexus, threatened to disrupt the global balance of power. At thirty-eight, he was worth billions, and it seemed he had nowhere to go but up.

Nexus was more than just a social media platform. It was a technological marvel, a seamless entanglement of interconnected data that held the potential to revolutionize communication, commerce and even warfare. But its true power lay in its capacity to track and analyze the movements of the world's nuclear submarines, a capability that could be weaponized in the wrong hands. Governments were scrambling to control this Pandora's box, but Thorne remained oblivious to the storm brewing around him. He was, in his own words, "a visionary," consumed by his relentless pursuit of technological advancement.

Delia had spent the day immersing herself in the minutiae of Thorne's life, dissecting his every online move, his every public appearance. He was a recluse, a self-made billionaire who preferred the solitude of his sprawling estate to the glitter of Silicon Valley. His public persona was that of a charming, philanthropic innovator, but behind the façade, Delia sensed a vulnerability, a hidden complexity that made him both fascinating and dangerous.

His online footprint was a testament to his brilliance and ambition. His tweets were a mix of technical jargon and cryptic pronouncements about the future of technology. His blog posts were a series of thought provoking essays exploring the ethical implications of his creations. Thorne believed in the transformative power of technology. He saw himself as a harbinger of a new world.

Delia wasn't buying it. There was something unsettling about his unwavering faith in technology, a blind spot that hinted at a deeper, darker truth. She delved into his past, scouring every available record, every public statement, every interview. She uncovered whispers of a tragedy, a personal loss that had shrouded Thorne in a veil of grief.

The Organization had labeled him a "threat," a man whose app had the potential to ignite global chaos. They were obsessed with the potential for Nexus to fall into the wrong hands, to be used as a tool of espionage and warfare. Delia understood their concerns, but there was something else, something that resonated within her. Her assignment was to eliminate Thorne and bring her client the app, but she wondered why, if the app was so dangerous, they didn't just destroy it. She was wondering if there was something else she wasn't a part of. In the past, that wouldn't have been a problem, but after the attack on Masters and the fact that they gave her more information than normal about this target, she wondered if she was being played, and she didn't like the feeling.

She studied Thorne's face, the lines etched by time and the weight of his achievements. His eyes, a deep emerald green, held a flicker of sadness, a reflection of a hidden pain. He wasn't just a tech titan, a brilliant visionary. He was a man, a man who had lost something precious, a man who was grappling with a secret that threatened to unravel his world.

As she stepped away from the window, the cityscape blurring into a sea of lights, Delia made a silent promise. She would eliminate Thorne, she would fulfill her mission, but not before she unraveled the truth behind his enigmatic façade.

She would learn his secrets, discover the darkness that lurked beneath his brilliance. This was more than just an assassination; it was a journey into the head of a man who held the power to change the world, a man who was himself a victim of the very technology he had created.

The next day, Delia woke to the sound of chirping birds, the sunlight streaming through the window. She moved through the day with a quiet grace, her every move calculated, her smile practiced. She was looking for an in. A way to get to Thorne and fulfill her assignment. She was a killer. One of the best in the business.

She spent the afternoon researching Thorne, delving into his online presence, his past, his relationships. She traced his path, piecing together the fragments of his life, searching for the key that would unlock his secrets. Her research led her to a digital forum dedicated to Nexus, a platform where his faithful followers and critics shared their thoughts, their anxieties, their hopes for the future of technology. It was in this digital labyrinth that Delia stumbled upon a thread, a post that mentioned Thorne's wife, a woman named Amelia, who had died in a car accident a year prior.

The post, written by a user who claimed to be a close friend of Thorne's, spoke of Amelia's warmth, her intelligence, her love for her husband. It described how Thorne had withdrawn into himself after her death, how he had become obsessed with his work, driven by a need to fill the void left by her loss. The thread also mentioned a rumor, a whisper about a secret that Thorne was keeping, a secret that was tearing him apart from the inside.

Delia's heart skipped a beat. This was the key she had been searching for. The secret that Amelia's death had unleashed, the darkness that lingered beneath Thorne's perfect life. She felt she might have found a way to get close to the reclusive billionaire. A way to break through his defenses and get close enough to kill him.

But how could she access this information without raising suspicion? How could she delve into Thorne's past without jeopardizing her mission? The man was a tech wizard. She had no idea if he had set up his personal internet to inform him when someone was looking into his life. The answer, she realized, lay in the digital world, in the vast expanse of the internet, where secrets were buried and truths revealed. Delia's eyes narrowed, a glint of steel flashing in their depths. She was a master of deception, a woman who could manipulate the shadows, a woman who could navigate the digital landscape with the same deadly precision she used in the real world. This was more than just a mission. It was a challenge, a test of her skills.

As the night descended, casting long shadows across her home, Delia slipped seamlessly into the role she had perfected. She was a phantom who moved unseen, unheard, through the digital world. She was a predator, stalking her prey. Her eyes focused on the prize, a truth hidden beneath the layers of Thorne's life.

| 6 |

The Perfect Façade

The scent of baked apple pie wafted through the air, a comforting aroma that seemed to cling to the very fabric of their suburban home. Delia, her long blond hair pulled back in a neat bun, arranged a bowl of fruit on the kitchen counter. The sunlight filtering through the window illuminated her features, highlighting the subtle lines that were etching themselves around her eyes, a testament to the relentless passage of time. From the outside, her life was a picture of idyllic normalcy. A loving husband, a flourishing career, a cozy home; a life that moved in predictable rhythms. Yet, beneath the façade, a different story unfolded.

Delia's world existed in stark contrasts. During the day, she was a high-powered lawyer, in demand by clients who were willing to pay for the best. By night, she shed the persona of lawyer and embraced a different identity, one that was forged in darkness and cloaked in shadows. Her true calling lay in a world where her skills were measured not in negotiating contracts and getting her clients out of trouble but in wielding weapons with deadly precision. She was a silent assassin who moved through the night with the grace of a predator and the precision of a surgeon.

She felt a strange pang of sympathy for the man, a man who was as much a prisoner of his own ambition as he was a master of his own destiny. But was this man a threat, or was he a pawn in a much larger game, a sacrifice to preserve a fragile equilibrium that threatened to shatter?

The phone rang, its shrill sound piercing the serenity of her office. The familiar code, a series of clicks and beeps, sent a jolt of adrenaline through her veins. It was the signal that brought her back to the stark reality of her double life. She answered the call, her voice calm, her demeanor composed.

"You have everything in place?" a voice whispered. It was the voice of the director, the man who had trained her, the man who saw her as a tool, a weapon.

"Everything is ready," she replied, her voice betraying no emotion. "He will be alone this evening. His security is substantial, but it will be a clean operation."

She could hear the subtle satisfaction in his voice, a satisfaction that lacked any emotion.

"Good. He is a liability, a threat to the world's stability. Don't hesitate. Execute the order."

The phone went dead. Most of the time, the decision to accept an assignment was an easy one. The person was notoriously bad: a terrorist, a drug dealer, a dictator. But this time was different. The image of the billionaire—his kind eyes, his gentle smile, his quiet contemplation— flashed in her mind. On the outside, he was none of those things, yet she knew looks could be deceiving.

Her life was a tapestry woven with threads of darkness and light, a symphony of conflicting emotions. In the twilight hours, she would have to make a choice. A choice that could alter the course of history, a choice that could define her destiny.

| 7 |

A Deadly Assignment

Alexander Thorne was a man who thrived in the shadows. His wealth had been amassed through ingenious algorithms and audacious business moves, and he'd built a technological empire from scratch. He was a genius, a visionary, yet his life was shrouded in secrecy, his personal life an enigma. The Organization had gathered little information about Thorne's habits, his routines, his predilections. His fortress was a sprawling estate on the California coast, guarded by state-of-the-art security systems. Yet, as with all targets, there were vulnerabilities, hidden pathways, and cracks in the armor.

Each new mission was like none that had preceded it. Every step was calculated, every move a risk. She knew the Organization expected precision and ruthless efficiency, and she had never failed them.

The instructions were precise, leaving no room for doubt. Gain access to Thorne's estate, eliminate the threat, retrieve the programming for the app and disappear without a trace. She was a master of her craft, and she was ready to execute the mission with the coldness she was known for.

As the sun set, casting long shadows across the California coastline, Delia prepared for her operation. Yet beneath the surface, there was a storm brewing. She knew she had to act, that the world depended on her. But as she drove towards Thorne's estate, the moon casting its ethereal glow on the road, she questioned her life choices. Perhaps she had been doing this for too long. She had taken the death of Robert Masters hard. Not because she had feelings towards him or his sons, but because she felt she had been used by the Organization. Her code of never killing innocents had been violated, and she wondered if it was time to find something else to make her life complete. She shook off the thought and focused on the mission.

Delia picked up her phone and dialed her husband. "Hi, honey. How's your day going?"

"Good, babe," said David. "This new project has hit a couple of hiccups, so I may be a little late tonight."

"That's okay. That's why I was calling. I just got a call from a client, and his son has gotten himself in trouble again. I need to see if I can get him released tonight, so I may be late. Don't wait up. There's an apple pie on the counter and steaks in the fridge."

She could almost hear David smile on the other end. "You're the best. Okay, take care of your client. You know they are lucky to have you. Love ya."

"Love you too," she said. She disconnected the call. She hated lying to David. She thought he deserved better. They had been married for more than a decade, and he'd never once questioned her late-night meetings or the time she would stay away from home, helping some client. She often wondered how he could be so trusting. Delia was gorgeous, yet he never questioned her, believing what she told him. She didn't deserve him, but she was lucky she had him. Delia turned off her phone and got ready to leave. It was time to prepare.

***

The gates to Thorne's estate stood like imposing sentinels guarding a world of privilege and power. Delia had parked her car a quarter mile down the road in a copse of heavy trees and bushes and made her way along the wall until she reached the spot she had determined would give her the best access to the estate. She climbed over the wall, just as she had practiced many times in her mind. The estate was a labyrinth of sprawling gardens, ornate fountains and breathtaking views. Thanks to her research and several internet satellite mapping programs she had access to, she knew every inch of the estate, and that would work to her advantage.

Working her way through the trees, she spotted the mansion, a sprawling edifice of glass and steel, its windows reflecting the moonlit sky. It was an impressive fortress, but Delia knew she could breach any security system, any barrier. She had honed her skills for years, perfecting the art of stealth, of infiltration, of becoming invisible. The target was close, yet a strange sense of unease crept over her. This was just another mission, yet the nagging thoughts of her last assignment that she had experienced earlier had returned. She had no idea where they came from, but she knew she had to put all her focus on the job at hand.

She checked her weapon, a custom-made silenced 22caliber semiautomatic pistol that held fifteen bullets made to her precise specifications. She made sure there was a round in the chamber and placed it back in her holster.

As she moved through the shadows of the estate, her senses were on high alert. She loved the tension in the air. The way it made her heart pound a little faster, the way the air seemed to crackle with anticipation. She knew she was close. She had prepared for every scenario, for every contingency.

Yet, something didn't feel right. There was a hidden dimension to this mission, a layer of complexity she hadn't expected. It wasn't just about eliminating the target; that was the easy part for her. What bothered her was why the Organization was so fixated on getting the app. She could just as easily destroy it, and then no one would have access to it. She wondered who the client was that was pushing for the retrieval. The Organization worked with clients all over the world, some good and some, well, not so good, but they had never taken on a mission for a client that might harm the United States. She wondered if that mandate had changed.

As she made her way towards the mansion, she knew she had to be careful. Her instincts were screaming at her to retreat, to abandon the mission, yet she felt compelled to continue.

Delia reached the mansion, her heartbeat slow and steady against her ribs. The shadows swirled around her, whispering secrets, urging her onwards. She moved with the agility of a panther, her movements a silent symphony of skill and grace. She had learned to blend with the darkness, to become one with the shadows, and she felt a sense of anticipation, a thrilling mix of fear and excitement.

Thorne's mansion was a fortress of security, every inch protected. But she had a plan, a strategy that had been meticulously crafted, and she was confident in her abilities. She had never come up against a security system she couldn't penetrate, human or machine, yet, this time, she felt a sense of vulnerability, a vulnerability that she had never experienced before. This mission, this target, had been condemned to death for a piece of software he created, yet the person she read about in the file didn't seem like he was a threat to anyone.

Delia pulled the lockpick kit from her pocket and pulled out two picks. She unlocked the door that led to the kitchen and pushed it open. She pulled her pistol and held it in front of her as she stepped into the kitchen. She had slipped past several of the exterior security guards while making her approach to the building, her movements as fluid as water, her presence invisible to all but the most keen observers. She moved through the mansion, her eyes adjusting to the darkness, her senses heightened, her mind racing. She had been trained for this, prepared for anything, yet she had a sense that something was amiss. Like in every mission before, she knew she was walking into danger.

She walked down the darkened hall and slipped into the first door on the right. She found herself in a large study, its walls lined with bookshelves, its desk cluttered with papers and electronic devices. A single lamp illuminated the room, casting long shadows that stretched across the floor. The room smelled of expensive cigars and aged leather, a reminder of the man who lived here. She could almost see him sitting at his desk, his face illuminated by the lamp, his eyes sharp, his mind working tirelessly.

Delia moved slowly, her eyes scanning the room, searching for any signs of movement. She knew she had to be careful. Thorne was not just a target, he was someone formidable. She could feel his presence in the room, his intelligence, his power. He was a master of technology, and she knew she had to be at her best.

She moved towards the desk, her hand reaching for the files that lay scattered across the surface. Her fingers grazed the top of a laptop. Delia opened the laptop, the screen illuminating her face with a cold blue light. She pulled a USB drive from her inside pocket and inserted it into the laptop. She pushed the tiny button on the end of the drive and a tiny red light lit up. She heard the laptop come to life. The red light turned green, and the laptop opened up to her.

Part of her assignment was to retrieve the program files for Nexus, and she scrolled through them, searching for the information she needed, including the evidence that would prove Thorne's true intentions. But as she read, a sense of confusion washed over her. The files didn't match the Organization's intelligence. They didn't paint Thorne as the ruthless, power-hungry mastermind they had described. Instead, they showed a man obsessed with innovation, with creating a better world, a man driven by a genuine desire to make a difference. Everything she read led her to believe that Thorne had no desire to sell the program to anyone, but wanted to release it as open source and put everyone in the world on an even footing, thus avoiding future wars and conflicts. That seemed kind of noble, she thought. Détente had worked during the Cold War. Why not now in this dangerous world they all lived in?

She shook off the thought. It wasn't her place to figure out the whys and the hows. That would be up to people way above her pay grade. She had two jobs to do, and as she downloaded all the program documents to her external hard drive, she knew it was time to move on to the second part of her assignment.

Something was nagging at her. Was Thorne the threat the Organization had made him out to be? Or was there something else at play, something she couldn't yet grasp?

She couldn't afford to make a mistake. But as she continued reading, a new understanding dawned on her. This wasn't about control, it was about the power of information, about who had access to it and who didn't.

Delia wondered if the Organization had twisted the truth to suit their own agenda, or if for a second straight time they had not fully vetted the mission. She felt as if they might be using her, exploiting her skills for a result she didn't yet know. But she wasn't just a pawn in their game. A strange thought occurred to her. She was a woman with a conscience, and she didn't like the idea that she was being used again.

The laptop screen flickered, the hum of the machine growing louder, and she felt a sense of urgency. Delia knew she had to get out of there, but first she had something she needed to do. But the more she thought about killing

Thorne, the more she wondered if it was the right thing to do. The questions in her mind were an unfamiliar experience for her. She had never doubted her determination to complete a mission, but suddenly, she wasn't sure. She wondered what would happen if she aborted the mission. If she gave them the program, would it be enough? She doubted it.

She knew the Organization would send someone else to kill him and probably her as well. She closed the laptop. She should never have read the files on the laptop. She had seen too much, learned too much. She had discovered a truth that could destroy everything she knew, everything she believed. She shook her head to clear her thoughts. She needed to find Thorne and complete the assignment.

Delia left the study, her steps silent, her movements swift. She searched the rest of the mansion, but she knew that if she didn't complete the mission, she would make an enemy of the Organization. But she was no longer afraid. She had a purpose now, a mission of her own. She would expose the truth, she would fight for justice, she would protect Thorne from the shadows that sought to destroy him. She had walked into a world of darkness, but now she was ready to shed light upon it, to fight for what was right, even if it meant defying everything she had ever known.

The search of the mansion turned up nothing. Thorne was not anywhere on the property. Was this another lie she had been fed? The information they had received should have been solid, that Thorne would be on the property. Yet as she made her way through the mansion, she found that information proved false. She wondered what the hell was going on. She felt like she was being set up to fail, and Delia Cahill didn't fail.

Delia reached the kitchen door. She knew she had to leave, that she had to escape, but she needed to make sure Thorne was safe. She had to warn him, to tell him the truth, to let him know he was in danger. But she also had to protect herself, to protect her identity, to stay one step ahead of those the Organization would send after her.

She took a deep breath, steeling her resolve. She had to do this, had to face the truth, to fight for what she believed in, even if it meant risking everything. Delia had come to this mansion to eliminate a threat, but she had discovered something far more dangerous, a conspiracy that went to the highest levels of power. She had been used, but she refused to be used any longer. She would expose the truth, no matter the cost.

As Delia slipped out of the mansion, the shadows closing in around her, she knew she was entering a world of danger, a world where there were no rules, no boundaries, no guarantees. She had a purpose, a reason to fight, and she was determined to see it through. This was a battle for justice, a battle for the truth, a battle for her own soul. And she wouldn't back down.

As she entered the trees, she looked back at the mansion, its windows reflecting the moonlit sky, its silhouette a beacon in the darkness. She knew Thorne was in danger, but she was determined to protect him, to help him, to become his ally in a world that was far more complex, far more dangerous than he probably ever imagined. This was a new mission, a mission of her own, and she was ready to face it, whatever the cost.

She reported back to the Organization that she'd had to abort the mission. Alexander Thorne was not at his estate. She didn't tell them she had the programing for the app, but something was nagging at her that she couldn't shake. It had all been too easy. What was she missing? She would hold on to that bit of information until it was necessary to reveal it. They would need a new plan. The longer she could keep the Organization in the dark about her plans, the better off she would be.

| 8 |

A Glimpse of Danger

Delia arrived home well after midnight and noticed that the lights were all off. David always turned on the front porch light when she was working late. She pulled into the garage, slid out of the car and reached behind her to make sure her pistol was in its usual spot. She entered the house from the garage and, leaving the lights off, made her way through the house.

Finding nothing out of order on the ground floor, she made her way up the stairs, stepping as close to the edge of each stair tread as possible to avoid any squeaks. She checked her office, David's office and the spare room. She pushed open the door to their bedroom and flipped on the light. Their king-sized bed was still made up, and the room was empty.

Delia was always concerned that someone from her past might find her and cause harm to David. She pulled her phone and opened the phone tracking app. She stopped and stared. David's phone was pinging off cell towers around Orange County. Nowhere near his office or their house.

She pulled up her map app and looked at the area. There were some mom-and-pop stores but not much else. Then she spotted something. There was a small bar called Jerry's Place.

Delia slipped into her office and opened up her desktop. She pulled up a program she wasn't supposed to have and entered the address of the bar. She hoped they had security cameras that were connected to the cloud. If they did, she could hack into the system and see what was going on. The location didn't have a listed security system, but she found several cameras that had a view of the front of the bar. She backed up the videos and watched. At 10 P.M. she spotted David walking towards the bar, but David was not alone. Walking next to him was a petite, dark-haired woman. She was hanging on his sleeve.

"What the fuck?" she said out loud.

Fury burned through her as she watched them enter the bar. She kept watching, and she spotted them leave. She checked the time stamp. Twenty minutes ago, they left the bar. They looked very cozy. She sat back in her chair.

"There must be a legitimate reason," she said, but she had no idea what that would be.

She turned off her computer, walked to her bedroom, disrobed and slid under the covers. She was mad as hell, but she would give him the benefit of the doubt. She owed him that much after all the lies she had told him over the years, but his lie hurt her deeply.

***

The hot, dry air of the California summer pressed against her skin, the scent of lavender and citrus heavy in the air. A light breeze blew off the Pacific Ocean and brought with it a freshness to the house in the hills above Los Angeles.

David lay beside her, snoring softly, his face illuminated by the faint glow of the morning sun. He looked peaceful, oblivious to the turmoil churning within her. Delia could smell the booze seeping out of his pores, so she slid out of bed, showered and put on her robe. She headed to the kitchen for coffee.

David Cahill, six foot and 190 pounds with blond hair and bright blue eyes, worked as a technology project manager for the Defense Department. He had graduated near the top of his class and had been recruited into the Defense Department right out of college. He was well respected by his peers and considered something of a prodigy in the world of cybersecurity.

Two hours later, he walked into the kitchen, wearing his typical business attire: jeans, button-down shirt and running shoes. He slipped up behind Delia and kissed her on the cheek. Delia turned from the stove and kissed him passionately. His hand reached under her purple robe, and she pushed his hand away.

"Breakfast is ready, and you'll be late," she said with a smile, turning back to the stove and turning off the burner. David slipped into his seat, and Delia placed a pile of scrambled eggs and three strips of bacon onto the plate. His coffee cup was filled and waiting.

"How did things go last night? Were you able to help your clients' kid?" he asked, placing a forkful of eggs into his mouth.

Delia sat next to him and buttered her toast.

"Everything was fine," she said. "You got in kind of late last night?"

David smiled. "Yeah, we had a good day, and the team went out for a couple of drinks. I knew you were gonna be late, so I went along. Just a bunch of the guys blowing off a little steam."

Delia couldn't understand why he lied to her. She would have believed anything he told her, but she knew the truth. They finished their breakfast with small talk about their plans for the day.

Delia walked David to the door and handed him his backpack. "Now, don't forget," she said, "I have that fundraising thing for one of my clients tonight, so I might be a little late."

David looked at her sideways. "Did we talk about that?"

"Yeah," she said with a smile. "About a week ago. You asked me what group the fundraiser was for, and I told you I couldn't care less, as long as the client was happy."

David nodded. "Okay, I must be getting old and forget-ful." He kissed her. "Have fun tonight. Love ya."

"Love you too," she said and closed the door behind him. Someday the lies would end. She hoped they wouldn't end with her life.

She sat in the kitchen and tried to understand what was happening in her life. First the Organization fucked her over twice, and now her husband was lying to her. She was feeling used, and she didn't like the feeling. She finished her coffee and got dressed. She needed to get her head in the game.

Tonight, the shadows beckoned. The text had come before she had gotten out of bed. The Organization had discovered that Thorne was to be the guest of honor at a fundraiser for a foundation his late wife had established. He was going to be honored for a donation made by the foundation that would add a new cancer center to a small inner-city clinic and would bring healthcare to thousands of cancer victims who would otherwise have to drive hours. The Organization contributed substantially in Delia's name so she could gain access to the event. Thorne hated these kinds of events, but he had agreed to honor his late wife. He had no way of knowing that this outing might also lead to his death.

Delia calmed her heart rate to a familiar drumbeat of anticipation. Her usual detachment, the clinical distance she maintained between herself and her targets, felt compromised. She had studied Thorne, gleaned information about him from various sources, and pieced together a picture of the man behind the genius. He was a man who built his world around the digital realm, choosing isolation over human connection. This lack of human interaction, amplified her sense of unease.

There was something about Thorne that resonated with her, something that sparked a flicker of understanding within her hardened heart. He was a man consumed by his work, a man driven by an insatiable thirst for knowledge, and in his pursuit of innovation, he had become a prisoner of his own creation. He reminded her of herself, of her self-imposed exile from the world, her commitment to a path that had demanded sacrifices and left her isolated.

Delia checked her watch and left her house, sliding into her SUV. It was time to slip into her secret world, shedding the façade of the mundane. The Organization had provided her with an apartment hidden in a quiet upscale neighborhood, miles from her house and her office, a place where she shouldn't run into anyone she knew. The apartment was her sanctuary, her haven from the world. The walls were lined with weapons, tools of her trade, each one a testament to her dedication.

She opened the closet and pulled out a stunning black evening gown that fit her like a glove, cut low enough to reveal her ample breasts and with a slit up the side that showed her incredible legs. The dress was designed to distract and yet make her memorable. Conflicts that would keep her safe. With no way to carry her pistol on her person, her weapon of choice was a composite knife strapped to her upper thigh. Otherwise, she would need to use her skills if the opportunity presented itself to take out her target, but before she decided, she still hoped to talk with him first. To find out what this man had done to cause people to fear him and want him dead, and what she could do to keep him alive.

The Organization had provided her with the details. The fundraiser would take place at the high-rise penthouse of Gordon and Elizabeth Simian. Gordon Simian was a successful hedge fund manager, and his wife was known for her philanthropic activities throughout the city. The setting wasn't ideal. The apartment overlooked the city, all the way to the ocean. The party, a throng of the rich and famous, and a target who would be distracted by his own brilliance might give her a chance to figure out what she was going to do.

Her plan was to move through the crowd, blend in, become invisible and then find an opportunity to talk to him. It was a routine she had performed countless times, a skill that she had mastered. Tonight, she needed to understand if there was something about her victim that made him dangerous or if she was being played. If she deemed him dangerous, then tonight he would die.

As she drove towards the apartment building housing the penthouse, the city lights blurred into a canvas of color, a tapestry of human activity that she was about to disrupt. Her pulse quickened as she reached her destination. The building stood tall and proud, a beacon of wealth and ambition. She parked a few blocks away, blending in with the other cars, and walked towards the building, her steps deliberate and confident.

The security was tight, but she had expected this. She moved through the checkpoints, her movements fluid and precise, her identity a mere whisper in the crowded lobby.

She reached the penthouse floor, a private world of opulence and extravagance. The door was ajar, the sound of music and laughter spilling out into the hallway, a cacophony of celebration.

Delia took a deep breath, her senses on high alert. She was about to enter the lion's den. And tonight, the lion was a man with a mind that could change the world, a man who, if she felt he was lying to her, would become her next victim.

She was prepared to eliminate a man who, despite his brilliance, was also human, a person who had stumbled upon a powerful truth, who she now realized bore an uncanny resemblance to herself. She was about to do what she had been trained for, what she was born to do. It was up to Alexander Thorne to convince her he was worthy of being kept alive. She stopped for a few seconds to clear her head of thoughts from a long time ago

Early Chapter

*T*he cool air of the attic sent shivers down her spine, a sensation that had nothing to do with the temperature. The dust motes danced in the weak light filtering through the grimy window, each speck a fleeting ghost of memories past. A young Delia stood before a dusty trunk, its worn leather surface etched with the scars of time, its brass clasps tarnished, yet holding a weight far heavier than their simple appearance suggested. It was a portal to a life she had tried so hard to bury, to forget, yet here it was, rising like a phantom from her past, demanding to be acknowledged.

Her fingers trembled as she reached for the clasps, the cold metal sending a jolt through her. She knew what she would find inside: a collection of photographs, letters and trinkets from her childhood, remnants of a life stolen from her before it began. A life she had abandoned, or rather, one that had been ripped away. The memories, like faded photographs, were still there, haunting her, demanding their rightful place in the tapestry of her existence.

As she pried open the trunk, the musty scent of forgotten times washed over her, a tangible reminder of the years she had spent running from her past, from the life that haunted her. She lifted the lid, her heart hammering against her ribs, each beat echoing the rhythm of a life lived and lost. There, nestled amidst layers of tissue paper, were the remnants of a childhood she barely remembered, a life before the shadows of her current existence had consumed her.

The photographs were the first to catch her eye. Her younger self, a smiling, carefree child, beamed back at her from the worn paper. It was a face she barely recognized, so different from the hardened mask she wore now. The girl in the photographs was innocent, oblivious to the darkness that awaited her, a darkness that would stain the fabric of her life.

She picked up a photo of her parents, their faces etched with a love that seemed impossible to comprehend now. Their smiles were genuine, unmarred by the tragedy that had taken them from her, leaving her adrift in a sea of pain and anger. The memories, like faded ink, had bled into one another, creating a blurry picture of their lives, of her life, before the storm.

The next photo showed her with her best friend, Sarah. Sarah's bright, mischievous grin mirrored her own. They were inseparable then, two young souls connected by a shared sense of adventure, oblivious to the cruel twist of fate that would tear them apart. Sarah had been the one who knew the real Delia, the girl beneath the manufactured veneer of perfection. The memory of her laughter, her unwavering loyalty, pierced the haze of her past, a bittersweet reminder of a life lost.

She lifted a small, worn teddy bear from the bottom of the trunk. Its fur was tattered, its button eyes faded, yet it held a weight far greater than its diminutive size. This was the bear her mother had given her on her fifth birthday, a symbol of innocence and comfort that had been stolen from her when her world shattered.

She could almost hear her mother's voice, soothing, as she whispered stories of a life filled with love and laughter. The memory of her gentle touch, the scent of her perfume, all of it came flooding back, a bittersweet torment that left Delia aching for a past she could never reclaim.

A bundle of letters, tied with faded ribbon, lay beneath the teddy bear. Her fingers traced the faded ink, and she recognized her father's spidery script, each letter a testament to his love and his hopes for a future that never came to pass. He had always been the quiet one, a man of few words, but he had a heart overflowing with love. His letters were filled with stories of his travels, of his work and, most important, of his unwavering love for his family. He had been taken far too soon, his laughter silenced, leaving a void that would remain in her heart.

She unfolded each letter, the words blurring through a veil of tears. She read them again and again, trying to absorb the warmth and love that emanated from the paper, a desperate attempt to hold on to a sliver of the life she had lost. The memories, raw and painful, threatened to consume her, but she couldn't let them. She had to face them, acknowledge them, even if it meant feeling the full weight of their pain.

As she read the letters, a realization dawned on her. The pain, the anger, the resentment she had carried for so long had become a prison, a cage that prevented her from living. She had spent years blaming herself, blaming the world for the tragedy that had befallen her family. But in those letters, she saw a different story, a story of love, resilience and hope.

Her parents had loved each other deeply, had cherished their family. They had faced adversity, had fought for a better life, and their love had never wavered, even in the face of death. In their letters, she found a sense of redemption, a reminder that even in the darkest of times, love and hope could endure. Delia closed the trunk, the weight of its contents settling like a heavy blanket over her soul. It was a burden she had carried for years, but in facing it, in acknowledging it, she had found a glimmer of light, a path to healing. She had faced her past, and, in doing so, she had let go.

As she descended the attic stairs, a sense of resolve filled her. She still carried the scars of her past, the indelible marks of the life she never knew.

| 10 |

First Encounter

The city lights below shimmered like diamonds on a black field. Delia stepped up to the massive glass wall and looked down to the streets below. The view of the city out one side was incredible, and the view to the west was a massive black void. Stars were visible high above the Pacific Ocean. The view was mesmerizing. She spotted the woman approaching, and instinct took over.

"I haven't seen you at one of my parties before." The woman, middle-aged and decked out with some of the most beautiful pieces of jewelry Delia had ever seen, held out her hand. "Elizabeth Simian, welcome to my home."

Delia turned. "Delia Cahill." She shook Elizabeth's hand. "Your home is stunning."

"The view never gets old," said Elizabeth. She looked at Delia with curiosity. "Delia Cahill. Would you be the lawyer to the rich and famous? That Delia Cahill?" "I guess I am," said Delia.

"Well," said Elizabeth. "It is indeed a pleasure to meet you. Your donation to the foundation this morning surprised us all. It's not often someone donates two hundred and fifty thousand dollars and isn't looking for something."

Delia's cheeks flushed. *So that's how I got the invite to the party. Two hundred and fifty K.*

"Your foundation supports many causes close to my heart. I know you will use the money wisely."

Elizabeth waved over a waitress carrying a tray of champagne glasses. She took two glasses and handed one to Delia. "A toast to a successful partnership."

They clinked the crystal glasses, and Delia sipped the champagne and smiled. Elizabeth looked up from her glass. She smiled as a man walked towards them.

"Ah, Alexander. Please meet Delia Cahill, a famous lawyer, and a wonderful benefactor to the foundation. Delia, Alexander Thorne."

Delia turned and found herself face-to-face with the man she had been assigned to kill.

"Miss Cahill," he said, his voice a low baritone that sent a shiver down her spine. His face was sculpted by time and etched with an enigmatic smile. He reached out his hand, and she took it. She could feel a strange warmth radiate through her body. His eyes, a deep, fathomless jade green, held a gaze that seemed to pierce through her façade.

Alexander Thorne was six feet tall and fit. His hair was black with a hint of gray, and it hung to his shoulders. The pictures of him that Delia had reviewed did not do him justice. He exuded confidence, and while everyone else in the room was dressed in evening wear, he wore jeans and a black T-shirt under a black leather blazer. He appeared to be a bit of a rebel, and he looked uncomfortable among all the glitz and glamour.

"Delia Cahill," she said. "Alexander Thorne. Why does that name sound familiar?"

Thorne seemed taken aback. He looked at her. She didn't appear to be the least bit impressed with him. He wasn't sure how to respond.

"Perhaps you have used some of my company's software products?" he said.

Delia smiled. "Perhaps, but I usually leave that stuff to my tech people. Are you a programmer?" she asked.

Alexander Thorne felt disarmed, his instincts faltering in the face of this enigmatic woman. Delia, a woman whose beauty was both striking and intimidating, adjusted the chain from the small black purse that hung from her shoulder and took a sip of champagne to steal a minute to compose herself.

"I own the company," he said, more sharply than he intended.

Delia laughed. "Relax, Mr. Thorne. I am teasing you. I know who you are, and it is a pleasure to meet you."

Elizabeth laughed, spotted someone across the room and excused herself, leaving Delia and Thorne standing by the window.

Delia broke the awkward silence. "Do you often come to affairs such as this?" she asked. "Everything I've read about you—which is not much, by the way—says you are a bit of a recluse."

Thorne smiled. "I always disliked that word, recluse. Makes me feel like a doddering old fool, hiding away from the public."

Delia raised her hand to her mouth. "I'm so sorry," she said. "It was not my intent."

Thorne cut her off with a wave. "Now I am teasing you, Miss Cahill. A recluse is what I am. I'm afraid I have very little use for most people and prefer my own company. And to answer your question, no, I do not attend functions such as this. Elizabeth is my older sister, so I make an exception for her."

"Must be a lonely life," said Delia.

"I have my work to keep me busy, and I prefer the solitude of my estate to all this fuss."

A man wearing a plain black suit approached Thorne and whispered in his ear. Delia spotted the earbud in his ear and the bulge under his arm. Thorne listened and nodded. The man stepped back and joined two others, a man and a woman, and they stood by.

"I'm sorry, Miss Cahill. My associate has informed me it is time to leave. I understand you represent some very wealthy individuals, and I might be in the market for a new lawyer to help me work through the negotiations for a new product I am working on. Would you be free for lunch tomorrow?" He didn't wait for an answer. "I will send a car to pick you up." He handed her his phone. "Please give me your address and be ready at eleven."

Delia entered an address into his phone and handed it back. He looked at the address and nodded. "Until tomorrow, then." He walked away, leaving Delia standing there wondering what had happened. She felt like she had lost control of the situation, and that was not something she was comfortable with.

Delia spent another hour mingling with the guests and then excused herself and left the party. Once outside, she took a deep breath and composed herself. The evening had not gone as she had planned, and she felt like she'd had no part in it. She hoped their lunch tomorrow would be enlightening. She smiled and headed for her car.

| 11 |

An Interesting Lunch

The car passed through the massive gates and pulled to a halt in front of the mansion. Her second visit in three days, but this time it was not clandestine. The driver slid out of the SUV, walked around and opened her door.

"He's expecting you," the driver, a man with a face like a weathered mask, spoke in a low, raspy voice.

The front doors opened, and a uniformed servant stood to the side. Stepping out of the car, Delia felt a chill, not from the morning's air but from the anticipation that clawed at her. Inside the entrance, a discreet army of black-clad security personnel pulsed with an unspoken tension. Her heartbeat quickened in a steady rhythm, a drumbeat of adrenaline fueling her resolve. She passed her purse through the X-ray machine and stepped through the metal detector. The level of security surprised her, and she was glad that all she carried was her composite knife strapped to her upper thigh.

Delia was escorted through the mansion towards an imposing wall of glass doors with a view of the Pacific Ocean beyond. As she stepped through the glass doors, she was drawn to the figure standing alone by a nearby fountain. Even with his back to her, his presence was commanding, his dark hair tousled by a gentle breeze. There was an aura of quiet power around him, something that intrigued her even as her instincts screamed danger. Her escorts stood nearby.

Alexander Thorne turned and faced her. He walked towards her and took her hand.

"Ms. Cahill," he said, "I am so very pleased you chose to join me. Welcome to my home."

Delia shook his hand and stepped towards the patio rail. She looked through the glass rail to the beach fifty feet below. The coast in this part of California was rugged and dramatic, and the view from the patio was no exception.

"I'm glad you invited me," she said.

A young woman in a maid's uniform stepped up with a tray and two glasses of champagne. Thorne picked up both glasses and handed one to Delia. She accepted it.

"Lunch will be served in a few minutes. In the meantime, let us enjoy the view," he said. "Tell me a bit about your background, Delia. May I call you Delia?" he asked.

Delia smiled and repeated the story of her life that she had told many times before. Of course, none of it was real, but she said it so convincingly that sometimes even she believed it. When she finished, she looked at Thorne and smiled. She was about to ask about his background when the bodyguard announced that lunch was ready. They set their glasses on the top of the rail and followed the guard through a massive dining room and into a more intimate space.

The dark wood-paneled room contained a small table for two, and the lighting made for an intimate setting. Delia scanned the room.

"The big dining room was something my late wife cared about. I prefer this small intimate space. Much more comfortable."

Much more intimidating, she thought.

He slid out one chair, and Delia sat. He slid in her chair, moved to the second chair and sat facing her. An older man stepped through a door at the end of the room and poured white wine into two glasses. This was followed by a server who entered with a beautiful salad and an assortment of dressings in small carafes. They ate in silence, as Thorne did not seem inclined to speak during the meal.

Once the meal—lobster served with an incredible pasta side dish and mixed vegetables steamed to perfection— was finished, Thorne pushed back his chair and leaned back.

"I hope everything was to your liking?" he asked. Delia nodded. "Everything was incredible." Thorne leaned in and smiled.

Delia looked into his eyes. "That's the second time you smiled like that. Am I missing something?"

He laughed. "I was thinking how incredibly beautiful you are and how well you delivered your life's story, almost like you've actually lived that life. Very impressive."

Delia felt a wave of discomfort flow over her. "I'm not sure I understand," she said.

Delia, her one hand under the table, reached under her skirt and touched the bottom of the knife on her thigh. She looked up as the door opened and two of the security guards stepped into the room and closed the door. She looked at Thorne.

"I would prefer you not reach for the knife under your skirt, Delia. We've been having too nice a time to have it end in tragedy. Please place both your hands on the table and enjoy the dessert."

He waved his hand, and the two security guards left the room. He picked up a small remote and pushed the button, and one of the wooden wall panels slid aside, revealing a large monitor. Pushing a second button, the screen filled with an image. An image she had not seen before but knew well. He pushed play and sat back and watched Delia as she moved through the office, sat at his laptop and plugged in the hard drive. He stopped the video.

"There's no sense going any further. We both know what happens and how this movie ends. It does not end, as we both know, with the theft of my programming code."

Delia was stunned, but she showed no emotion as she watched the video. She took a few bites of the tiramisu and put down the fork.

"Your AI is very good. That's an excellent likeness of me."

Thorne laughed.

"My dear," he said with a smile. "Did you think you could outwit the security system of a man the tech world calls a visionary? We had you on camera from the moment you climbed over the wall."

Delia sat back in her chair. She smiled. She now understood why something didn't feel right the other night. Someone had alerted him to her plans, and she would struggle with that, but not right now. Thorne stared at her.

"Why do you smile?" he asked.

Delia leaned forward. She picked up the fork and took another bite of the tiramisu. "It took three point five seconds from the time you pushed the button under the table for your security guards to enter the room." She waved the fork in front of her. "In that amount of time, I can shove this fork into your jugular, and in less than thirty seconds, you will die here at the table." She took another bite of the tiramisu and smiled.

Thorne lost some of his bravado and looked towards the door, then back to Delia. He was quiet for a minute. Delia could see his mind working.

He sat back in his chair and laughed. "Well done, Ms. Cahill. Well done. For a thief, you sound very knowledgeable about death. I believe you would have no problem doing exactly what you just suggested. I am impressed."

"Good," said Delia. "Then let's stop the dance; tell me why I'm here."

"All that information you pulled off my laptop was meant for you to find. None of it is real."

"Of course it's not real," said Delia. "You have the best security system money could buy, yet I found so many holes in it the night before last that, if it was my system, I would have fired the designer. But you are the designer, so that's not an actual option. My guess is you were sitting in your safe room with all your interior staff, watching the entire thing. So let's stop playing who's smarter and tell me what you're after."

"I understand you have a message for me," he said, his voice smooth as silk. "A message that could be interpreted as a threat."

Delia, her tone cold and professional, said, "Mr. Thorne, your app has caught the attention of certain . . . entities. They are concerned about the potential consequences of such technology falling into the wrong hands. My job the other night was to retrieve the Nexus program."

"I am aware of their concerns," Thorne said, his smile widening. "But I assure you, Nexus is a tool for progress, not destruction."

She studied him, his face a mask of contradictions. He was a brilliant innovator, a visionary who sought to reshape the world, yet he was surrounded by an aura of danger. There was something about him, a hint of vulnerability beneath the surface, that resonated with a part of her she had long suppressed.

Delia shifted in her chair, her senses alert, her mind clear. She was focused on her mission. She couldn't let this enigmatic man distract her, not when the world's fate hung in the balance.

"That may be true," Delia said, her voice laced with skepticism. "But there are those who believe otherwise."

"Those who see Nexus as a weapon, not a tool," said Thorne.

"That's correct, Mr. Thorne, which is why you are still alive," said Delia.

Thorne's smile faltered, replaced by a flicker of something that could be interpreted as fear or, perhaps, a hint of sadness. He looked deep into her eyes, his gaze intense, his voice lowered to a conspiratorial whisper. "You are study-ing me. There is something about your assignment that isn't sitting well with you, and you are deciding whether or not you will fulfill your assignment."

"You're very astute, Mr. Thorne," she said. "Had they sent anyone else, you would be dead already, but I'm not con-vinced that you are the evil bastard they seem to think you are. You need to convince me I am right."

For the first time since she had arrived, Thorne was at a loss for words. He sat still, his finger hovering over the se-curity button under the table. He raised his hands and placed them on the table. "What if I call the police and turn you and the tape over to them?"

Delia sat back in the chair. She held her hands out in front of her. "Please do, sir, so we can end this charade."

Thorne smiled. No one had ever spoken to him like that. He was shocked and intrigued. "I believe we share a com-mon enemy. Perhaps we could find a way to work together."

Delia felt a prickling sensation at the back of her neck, a warning that resonated with her killer instincts. This man was not a victim; he was a player in a contest far larger than she could comprehend. He was playing her, manipulating her, and she needed to be careful. Thorne was good. Very good, but Delia Cahill was better. She needed Thorne to convince himself that they should work together.

"I don't make deals," she said, her voice cold. "My focus is on the mission."

Thorne's eyes, those deep pools of jade green, held a flicker of disappointment. "Then I must convince you that your mission is wrong," he said, his voice regaining its cool composure. "My life's work is not for sale. But if you're looking for a way to protect your interests, I have a proposition for you."

He rose from his chair, stepped to the bar and poured two drinks, one of which he handed to Delia, his presence both intimidating and alluring.

"I have information," he whispered, leaning in so close Delia could feel the warmth of his breath on her skin. "Information that could make or break your mission. But you'll have to play my game to get it."

The air crackled with unspoken tension, the scent of his cologne, a blend of musk and citrus, invading her senses. She felt a surge of emotions: fear, curiosity and a burgeoning sense of danger that was both thrilling and terrifying.

Delia had never encountered anyone quite like Alexander Thorne. He was a nerd who could challenge her. Alexander Thorne was a puzzle, a riddle she desperately needed to solve.

"Your proposition," she said, her voice wavering, "it might be of interest. But I need a guarantee."

Thorne's smile returned, a flicker of amusement in his eyes.

"Guarantees are for fools," he said, his voice low and seductive. "But trust me, Delia, you'll be the one with the upper hand. And if you play your cards right, this might not be the only time we play together."

He turned away, but Delia's focus remained on the enigmatic billionaire. She was intrigued, but she still needed to know more if she was going to abort the mission. She wondered what was next.

The mission, the weight of the world resting on her shoulders, felt heavier than ever. She stood and followed him through the house, towards the front door. He reached out and took her hand.

"This has been a most interesting lunch, Ms. Cahill. Please allow me a little more time, and I will convince you that my intentions are truly honorable. Until next time." He kissed her hand and opened the door. Delia stepped through into the sunlight and walked to her car.

This wasn't just another assignment; it was the beginning of something far more complex. Delia Cahill, the world-class assassin, was about to enter a game she didn't understand, where the stakes were higher than life itself, and that might get her killed.

| 12 |

Beneath the Surface

Delia sat at her kitchen table and ran through the lunch she'd had with Thorne. She picked up her coffee cup and took a sip. She was concerned. Thorne had a video of her breaking into his house, yet he didn't have her arrested. He had set up fake files on a backup laptop so she could steal the documents. She had assumed the files were fake, but she wasn't sure what he was playing at. He knew his life was in danger, but he seemed unafraid. But what she couldn't quite work out in her head was why. He appeared to not know her actual assignment. There were two, possibly three people who knew her mission. *What the hell was he playing at and what did he want from me? Why didn't he call the police when he knew I broke into his house?*

She realized that their first encounter had been a mere formality, a staged introduction at a gala filled with the crème de la crème of society. With the polite smiles and forced conversation, Delia never sensed the flicker of recognition in his eyes. It was as if he saw through her façade, glimpsed the steel beneath the satin.

He was a man who kept his life shrouded in secrecy. Rumors of his past, his childhood, his rise to prominence, were whispered in hushed tones, a tapestry of half-truths and speculation. He lived in a world that worshipped at the altar of fame. The media clamored for a glimpse behind the iron curtain of his life, but he remained elusive, in their relentless pursuit.

Delia, trained in the art of deception, found herself intrigued. His reclusive nature, the air of mystery that surrounded him, was a challenge, a puzzle she couldn't resist piecing together. She had a job to do, a mission to fulfill, but the mission was compromised. She felt like she was stuck in a situation that she had little control over. If Thorne was telling the truth, that he had no interest in selling the app to the highest bidder, then he was worthy of saving. But she also wondered if he already had a buyer and was ready to make a deal. If that was the case, then she would need that information so she could stop the transfer. Either way, this mission had gotten bigger than first described. The man behind the app, the man who could hold the world in his hands, intrigued her.

His past was a story of loss and sacrifice, interwoven with an unwavering commitment to a world free from the scourge of war. But the flames of his past still flickered within him, a constant reminder of the price he had paid for his ambition.

Delia, the professional assassin, the woman who had mastered the art of detachment, found herself drawn into the vortex of his emotions. She saw the pain etched in his eyes, the unspoken burdens he carried. She recognized the vulnerability beneath his façade, the longing for connection in a world that sought to consume him.

As she delved deeper, she discovered a maze of secrets, a history that extended beyond the borders of his public persona. There were whispers of a past love, a betrayal that had left scars on his soul. His family was a shadowy presence in his life, a constant source of both support and suspicion. He was a man who walked a tightrope, balancing his past with the burden of his future.

And Delia, caught in the cross fire of his ambition and her own internal conflict, found herself torn. But the more she learned about him, the more she questioned why the people she worked for wanted him dead.

He seemed drawn to her, his guarded demeanor softening in her presence. He saw beyond her persona, glimpsed the woman beneath the armor. Saw the strength and the vulnerability, the compassion and the darkness, the duality that made her who she was. He recognized her as a kindred spirit, a soul who understood the weight of secrets and the price of ambition.

Delia was caught in a maelstrom of emotions, a battleground of loyalty and trust. Her world, once divided between her two lives, was now chaotic. She was torn between the oath she had sworn to the Organization and the growing interest she felt for Thorne. Twice the Organization had lied to her, and then her husband had lied to her. She wasn't sure what was going on, but her world seemed to be coming apart, and she wasn't sure who she could trust anymore.

Her mission had become blurred. She had to choose, to decide where her loyalties lay. The path ahead was shrouded in uncertainty, a treacherous journey with no guarantees. And as she stood on the precipice of her decision, she knew the consequences would be farreaching, the ramifications profound.

The world was a stage, and Delia, the woman with a double life, was playing a part she never expected. But she would maintain control. Her decision to kill or save Thorne would be on Thorne himself. She was running out of time.

| 13 |

Unraveling Secrets

The ringing phone snapped her out of her melancholy. She picked up the phone.

"Yes, sir," she said.

"Delia, is it done?" asked the director. She could tell from the tone of his voice that he was not pleased and that he also knew the answer to the question before he asked it.

"No, sir. There's been some complications."

"What complications, Delia?" asked the director.

"Well, sir. His security is much more complex than we expected. I need more time to get him alone."

"Delia, you have had three opportunities to complete the mission. Once at his home, the second time at a gathering for his sister's foundation, and again at lunch yesterday. Why didn't you do it yesterday at lunch?"

"We were never alone, sir. His security people watch him like a hawk, and his electronic surveillance is better than anything I have seen. I need a little more time to get close to him."

"Is there a problem, Delia? Do I need to hand over the assignment to someone else?"

"No, sir. I have never failed to complete an assignment, and I don't intend to fail this time."

"You've got forty-eight hours to complete the assignment. Get it done, Delia. I am also texting you a name and address. I don't want to know what happens next."

The director disconnected the call, and Delia sat at the kitchen table sipping her coffee. Her phone chimed with an incoming text, which she opened, looking at the number. She knew what the number was for. Now she had to do something about it. As soon as she was done with Thorne, she would deal with this.

Thorne was a manipulator, that was obvious, but was he trying to play her, or was he trying to save his own life? She was concerned that he was so well aware of her assignment that he had taken time to compile fake programming files and stage an entire break-in. What was he trying to prove? She finished her coffee and stood. If she couldn't figure out what was going on, then she would complete the assignment as ordered. End of story.

Her phone chimed with an incoming text message: *We need to talk. Car will pick you up in one hour. T.*

She grabbed a shower and got dressed. She strapped the composite knife to her thigh under her skirt. She had no idea why Thorne wanted to see her, but she hoped this meeting might lead to the information she needed.

***

The director placed his phone on the desk and looked at the man sitting across from him. He reached down and spread out the pictures on his desk. He looked at them for a minute.

"They seem pretty cozy," said the director.

"Yes, sir. Maybe too cozy. What do you want to do?"

The director stared at his guest. "We'll give her the forty-eight hours. If Thorne is still alive, then we'll bring in a team and take them both out. I'm not sure what's going on in her head, but this is not usual."

There was a knock at the office door, and a tech stepped into the office.

"Sirs, she just got a text from Thorne. He is calling her to another meeting."

The director nodded, and the tech left the office, closing the door.

"Does that change anything?" asked the guest.

"Have her followed and let's see what happens. I want to be certain before I commit to an action against her."

***

The elevator doors slid open, revealing a cavernous space bathed in the cool, sterile glow of minimalist design. Stepping out into the opulent expanse, Delia felt a shiver run down her spine. It wasn't the cold; it was the oppressive air of power, the palpable weight of a life lived in constant vigilance.

Her target stood at the far end of the expansive room, silhouetted against a panoramic view of the city. His back was to her, his broad shoulders taut, like a coiled spring. He wore tight jeans and a black T-shirt that hugged his imposing frame. His hair, a dark, unruly mane, seemed to defy the rigid order of his surroundings.

Even from a distance, she felt his presence, a palpable aura of intensity that crackled in the air around him. He was a predator, she knew it, but she would not be his prey. He turned, his gaze meeting hers with a disconcerting intensity. His eyes, a deep, impenetrable green, held a quiet strength. His lips, full and slightly parted, hinted at a hidden vulnerability, a stark contrast to the hard lines of his face. Yet, the entire scene felt staged for her benefit.

"Welcome, Delia," he said. He spoke in a smooth, cultivated tone, devoid of any discernible accent, yet it carried a faint hint of something . . . foreign, perhaps.

She managed a smile. "What is this place?" she asked, her eyes taking in her surroundings, noting all the escape routes. The four armed security guards never ventured farther than a few feet from his side. They watched her like prey watches the approaching lion, but this prey was ready to fight to protect their master.

"This is where I come to work when I need to be alone," he said, his voice laced with a subtle amusement. He walked towards her, each measured step resonating with a purpose.

His movements were slow, controlled, like a panther stalking its prey. He stopped a few feet away, his penetrating gaze holding her captive. She felt the tension in the room tightening with each passing second.

"Delia," he said, savoring the name on his tongue. "You're a woman of many faces, aren't you?"

His words were a veiled accusation, a challenge that sent a jolt through her person. She knew this man was dangerous, not just because of the power he wielded, but because of his ability to see through people, to sense the darkness that simmered beneath the surface of their ordinary lives.

She pushed back to regain control. "We all have our secrets, Mr. Thorne."

He chuckled, a low, throaty sound. "I wouldn't know, Ms. Cahill. I'm not in the business of secrets."

He smiled, his words masking a threat, a reminder of the power he held over her. She knew this game, the deadly dance of power and deception. She had played it before, but never with a man like Thorne.

He gestured towards a luxurious leather chair with a dismissive wave of his hand. "Have a seat, Delia. We have much to discuss."

She sat, calm, composed, and in control. She reached for the crystal glass of champagne that appeared on the table beside her.

"What is it you want to discuss, Mr. Thorne?" she asked, her voice steady but her mind racing with a thousand questions.

"Everything," he said, his gaze fixed on her, intense and unwavering. "You asked me to prove my intentions."

He leaned back in his chair, his posture relaxed yet radiating power. She felt a surge of adrenaline, a primal instinct to fight, to escape. But the allure of this enigmatic man, the danger that crackled around him, was too potent to resist.

"We all have secrets, Delia," he said, his voice dropping to a seductive whisper. "You're not the only one playing a game."

He leaned forward, his eyes boring into hers. "And in this game, Delia, there are no winners, only survivors."

He paused, allowing his words to sink in. Then he reached out, his hand hovering just above the glass, as if testing the air around her.

"Let's see how well you survive," he said, his voice a chilling promise.

As she reached for her glass, she knew that the game had begun.

Thorne remained an enigma, a shadow figure shrouded in mystery. He was a master manipulator, playing his cards close to his chest, leaving her guessing at his motives. He was a whirlwind of contradictions, charming one moment, cold and calculating the next. He was a man who could make you feel you were the most important person in the world, yet he could also leave you humble, like you were nothing but a pawn in his intricate contest.

Her attempts to uncover his secrets were met with a wall of impenetrable silence. He would offer tantalizing glimpses into his life, hinting at a past shrouded in darkness, but he always stopped just short of revealing anything substantial. It was as if he was playing with her. A battle where he was both the hunter and the prey.

While sipping a glass of champagne in the spartan surroundings of his penthouse, she decided to make a direct approach.

"You're good at keeping secrets," she said, trying to sound nonchalant.

He smiled, a wry twist of his lips that didn't reach his eyes. "Everyone has secrets, Delia. It's what makes us human."

"And what about you?" she asked, her voice laced with a dangerous edge. "What secrets do you hold?"

He settled back in his chair, his gaze sweeping across the city skyline. "My secrets are not for public consumption," he said, his voice a low purr that sent shivers down her spine.

"I know you're hiding something," she said, her voice steady but her heart pounding in her chest. "I can feel it. Why are you so afraid to let me in?"

"Afraid?" he scoffed, a touch of amusement lacing his voice. "I'm not afraid of you, Delia. I'm afraid of what you might discover."

He paused, his gaze intense, unwavering.

"I have lived a life of shadows," he continued, his voice low and husky. "A life where trust is a weakness and vulnerability a fatal flaw. I've built my world on secrets, on deception, on the illusion of control. And I don't want to lose it. Not to you, not to anyone."

His words connected with her on a deep level, a flicker of understanding. But Thorne was different. He was a man who lived in the shadows, who understood the darkness that lived within us all.

Delia stood up and looked out the window. She turned and faced him. "Let's stop the bullshit," she said. "You think you're playing some kind of mind game? Well, here's some facts. I told you to convince me you were righteous and were going to do good with your app. So far, all I hear is bullshit. You can play your game with me, but at some point, someone is going to kill you for your app. I might be able to help you, but so far, all you've convinced me of is that you're a slimy little man with a big ego." She looked at her watch.

"You've got five minutes. When I walk out that door, all bets are off. Do you understand?"

He met her gaze, his expression unreadable. For a moment, she thought she saw a flicker of something in his eyes, a vulnerability that had been guarded.

"You're asking for something dangerous, Delia," he said, his voice a husky whisper. "Something that could change everything."

"And I'm willing to take the risk," she replied. "If, in fact, you are the man I think you are."

His gaze was intense, his fingers tracing the rim of his glass.

"I'm not sure you're prepared for what you might find," he said. A chill ran up her spine.

As he raised his glass to his lips, she knew she had just stepped onto a path that would lead her deeper into the shadows, deeper into the heart of a secret that could shatter her world.

| 14 |

Conflicting Emotions

Thorne reached across the table and picked up her glass. "Follow me. I want to show you something. Something I don't share with many people."

He stood and walked towards the back of the penthouse. Delia stood and followed, unsure of where he was taking her. None of his security detail followed. Perhaps it was time to complete her assignment. She could feel the knife pushing against her thigh. It gave her a sense of control, even though she felt like she wasn't in control of anything. Perhaps she should just finish the job and move on before things got out of hand. But Thorne intrigued her, and she wanted to know more about him. She was breaking all the rules she had established over the years—allowing herself to get close to the victim. She wasn't sure why.

Thorne stopped before a vault door, entered a code in the panel next to the door and then leaned in as red beams moved over his eyes. The door clicked, and he pulled it open, revealing the vast expanse of his private art gallery.

The silence was broken by the soft hum of the ventilation system and the rhythmic ticking of a grandfather clock in the corner. The billionaire, his face obscured by the shadows, gestured towards a painting of a stormy seascape. A white cottage with blue trim, somewhere along the California coast.

"My father," he said, his voice a low rumble, "was a passionate collector. He believed art held the power to express the soul, even when words failed."

Thorne's company was built on a foundation of cuttingedge technology, a world diametrically opposed to the delicate world of art.

"It was his way of communicating," he said, his gaze lingering on the painting. "A way of expressing the complexities of life, the emotions that words often struggle to capture."

His words struck a chord within her. She too lived one life defined by cold, measured actions and another cloaked in a veil of normalcy. She was a master of disguise, a chameleon who adapted to her surroundings with an unsettling ease. Yet, there was a part of her, a hidden corner of her soul, that was seeking something more.

"It's . . . beautiful," she whispered, her eyes drawn to the painting's swirling colors and stormy sky. It was as if the painting reflected her own turbulent inner world, the tempest of conflicting emotions raging within her.

"It reminds me of you," he said, his voice a soft whisper that sent shivers down her spine.

The statement hung in the air, heavy with unspoken implications. Delia could feel a blush creep up her cheeks, betraying the turmoil within.

"How so?" she asked. Thorne's words were like a brushstroke across a canvas, painting a picture of her own inner world, a world she had kept hidden.

"You are like the storm," he continued, his gaze unwavering. "Powerful, unpredictable, with a depth that belies your outward appearance."

Delia smiled. Was he playing with her, toying with her emotions? Or was this something more, his attempt at connecting with his executioner?

Yet, his sharp intelligence and hidden depths were chipping away at her resolve, creating a dangerous crack in her façade.

She was a seasoned assassin, trained to shut down her emotions and execute her targets with clinical precision. But Thorne was different. He was a visionary, and he could prove to be a benefit, if he could be controlled.

He had a vulnerability, a loneliness that echoed her own. He was a man who hid behind walls of his own making, a fortress of technology and innovation that shielded him from the world. But she saw through his defenses.

"The storm can be destructive," she said, her voice hard. "A force of nature that shapes the world around it."

She could feel his gaze upon her, intense and penetrating. He seemed to read her thoughts, understanding the conflicting emotions that churned within her.

"You are not a storm," he said, his voice soft. "You are a woman who is trying to find her way, a woman who is fighting for a cause she believes in."

She looked at her watch. "You have one minute and I'm gone. The chips will fall where they may."

His words, though simple, resonated with a profound understanding. He wasn't judging her, wasn't condemning her for her actions, but saw her for who she was, a woman torn between two worlds, a woman caught in the cross fire.

"Why are you doing this?" she asked, her voice firm. The question was directed at him, but it was also a question she asked herself every day. Why did she live this life, a life of secrets and betrayals?

Thorne turned away, his gaze fixed on the stormy seascape. "Because I believe in what I've created, in the power of my technology to make the world a better place."

His words were a testament to his unwavering belief, a belief that echoed the conviction that had driven her to this point. But there was also a hint of desperation in his voice, a craving for something other than the sterile world of technology and innovation.

"You asked me to prove to you that my life was worth saving. There's no way I can do that. It's like trying to prove a negative. I want to make the world a better place. I have more money than God. I don't need to sell this app. If I release it as an open-source app, every country, every entity in the world, will have access to it. It will be like the Cold War all over again. No one will make a move without the others knowing about it. The world's enemies will be at a standstill. My goal is to make the app even better, so no one group can ever hold anyone else hostage. My father spoke through his art collection. I speak through my apps."

Delia felt a chill run down her spine. His comment and justification were designed to create sympathy. She thought about her own life. She could give him a dozen answers, a dozen justifications for the path she had chosen, but none of them would capture the complexity of her motivations.

"I . . . I'm trying to protect the world," he said, his voice trembling. "To prevent chaos, to ensure a future for humanity."

Delia knew the words were a lie. An attempt at sounding convincing. Even faced with a last-minute pitch to save his life, he still played the game. Delia was a weapon, a tool wielded by those in the shadows, a force of destruction disguised as a protector. Yet, in that moment, with his gaze upon her, she could have believed the words he was saying.

"And what about you?" he asked, his voice soft, yet filled with a power that resonated within her. "What are you trying to protect?"

His question pierced into her defenses. She had always been a protector, a warrior fighting for a cause she believed in. But what was her cause?

She struggled to answer, to articulate the complexities of her existence. A week ago, she knew exactly what she was fighting for, but now she wasn't so sure.

"I . . . I don't know," she whispered. The words were a confession, a revelation of the inner turmoil that raged within her.

"Maybe," he said, a gentle smile gracing his lips, "you're trying to protect yourself."

"Maybe," she whispered, the word carrying the weight of a thousand unsaid emotions. Delia felt a strange sense of liberation, as if a weight had been lifted from her shoulders. This man wasn't her enemy. He was a soul seeking solace, a beacon of hope in a world where darkness had become her reality and her job was to strike down that hope, but for the first time in her life, she questioned why.

She moved a few paces to her left and cast her eyes upon another painting even more beautiful than the last. She was so caught up in its beauty she never sensed him move.

Delia turned, and he was there. She froze as he leaned in closer and took her in his arms. Their lips touched, and he pulled her closer. Her body tensed as his tongue probed her mouth, and she responded in kind. Her body tingled, and she could feel the heat rise and threaten to consume her. She felt his hands as they moved down her back, sliding ever so gently, and the passion grew. Then reality reared its head and Delia pushed him back.

"No," she said. "I need to leave."

She walked past him, through the main room, to the elevator. She was confused. Her anger at the Organization and, more important, at David, had made her vulnerable, and Thorne had tried to take advantage of that. She hated him for who he was, but she had decided to help him. She believed that deep down inside was a guy who meant what he said. Only time would prove her right or wrong. She knew she was putting her life on the line, but she had made up her mind. She would abort the mission and protect him from anyone they sent after him.

Delia stepped into the elevator. She didn't like what had just happened, but she knew she needed to put some distance between herself and Thorne.

As the elevator descended, she leaned against the wall, her mind reeling. She had come to this penthouse with a clear mission, but now everything had changed. She had made a decision that would put her at odds with a powerful organization. An organization that she no longer believed was on the side of good. She had put her life in Thorne's hands, and all she could do now was wait for him to do the right thing.

She exited the elevator and made her way out of the building, needing the cool night air to clear her head. As she walked, she tried to make sense of the whirlwind of thoughts and emotions that were consuming her. Delia was pissed. She was pissed at the Organization for using her to take a life that was decent, and she was pissed at David for lying to her. She felt betrayed, and her answer to that betrayal was to betray everything she held dear. She wondered if there was a life outside of the world she lived in. A normal life she could never have.

Delia walked aimlessly, her mind a tumult of conflicting thoughts. She had always prided herself on her ability to remain dispassionate, to execute her assignments with precision. But this past week had shaken her to her core, causing her to question her purpose and her very identity.

As she wandered the city streets, the cool night air did little to calm her racing thoughts. She felt vulnerable. The kiss replayed in her mind. The sensation of his lips on hers had sparked something she had only felt with David. She had lost herself for the moment, but then was repulsed by her reaction. Thorne was a user and a manipulator, and she had let down her guard. That would never happen again. She had made up her mind. She would do everything she could to help Thorne bring his app to the free market, but then she was gone. There would be no going back to the Organization. And as far as David . . . she would need to see where that fell in her plan, but for now, she had a job to do.

The assignment now felt more complex and treacherous than before. Thorne was no longer her target, a name on a list. He was her protectee, and she needed to be on her A game.

Delia knew that not completing her mission would be a challenge, not just professionally but also personally. It would also be deadly. She didn't know of anyone who had quit the Organization. She was drawn to Thorne's vision for the future, and she would be there to make sure that vision came to fruition. Now she needed an escape strategy.

Delia's mind raced as she made her way through the city streets, the memory of Thorne's kiss still burning on her lips. The billionaire had awakened something in her she had already been considering: a desire to shed the shadows and step into the light. But was it worth the cost? Was it possible to walk away from her life of secrecy and betrayal?

Her mission had changed, and Delia knew that returning to her handlers and confessing her doubts would be dangerous, perhaps even deadly. She was alone in this struggle, caught between her duty and her desire for a different life.

| 15 |

An Unexpected Ally

Delia's steps slowed as she wandered along the path, her mind in turmoil; her thoughts kept returning to the art gallery. The soft hum of the ventilation system, the ticking of the grandfather clock and the beauty of the artwork combined to create a space that felt like a sanctuary. It was as if the art, with its ability to express the soul, had shown her a glimpse of a different life. A life where she could be more than just an assassin, a weapon in someone else's hands. A life where she could find solace and, perhaps, even redemption. But was it just an illusion? Was she fooling herself into believing that she could escape her dark reality?

The reality of her situation loomed over her, a constant reminder of the danger she was in. Thorne, enigmatic nature, was still a target, just not for her. The weight of her choice not to complete the assignment rested on her shoulders as she continued to walk, her mind settling into the decision she had made.

Delia's steps led her to the river, the moonlight reflecting off the gentle ripples. The city felt alive, its heartbeat pulsing through her veins. She felt melancholy— a dangerous feeling for an assassin, one that could get her killed. But it was also exhilarating, like a drug that she couldn't resist.

She knew that returning to her old life was impossible, but was stepping into the light a viable option? Could she leave the shadows behind? Or would she spend the rest of her life running and hiding? And what about the life she had made with David? Could she throw that all away on a whim? She wasn't sure why he had lied to her, but she loved him, and if there was a way, she would figure out how to take him with her, wherever her new life would take her.

As she gazed into the watery depths, she saw a reflection of herself—a woman standing at a crossroads. When faced with the decision of continuing in her life or moving on, she chose a fresh start, a chance to be free from the chains of her deadly profession. She knew the consequences, the dangers she would be facing, but she was ready to move forward with her life. All she needed to do to make it worthwhile and to validate her decision was to keep Thorne alive long enough to release his app. Then she would disappear into the shadows.

Thorne, with his mysterious past and captivating presence, held the key to her future. Yet the path forward remained obscured, shrouded in uncertainty and intrigue.

Delia stood there, transfixed by her reflection in the river, as if the water held the answers she sought. The moonlight cast an ethereal glow upon the scene, adding to the surreal nature of her dilemma. She knew that her life hung in the balance and the choice she'd made would shape her destiny. The thought of turning her back on her mission, of defying her handlers, was both empowering and petrifying. It was a prospect that simultaneously thrilled her and froze her to the core.

Delia's mind whirred as she grappled with her decision. The prospect of a normal life, free from the shadows and secrecy, was alluring. But it was also a life she had never known, and the unknown was treacherous terrain for an assassin like herself.

Was it possible to escape the chains of her deadly profession, or would they forever bind her, no matter where she went? The reality of her situation loomed, a constant, menacing presence.

As Delia stood at that metaphorical crossroads, the city's heartbeat pulsing in time with her own, she knew that her choice would shape her future and the fate of those around her. Yet the destination remained obscured, veiled in the same shadows that had both protected and entrapped her for so long. She took a deep breath, steeling herself for whatever lay ahead. With a final, lingering glance at the river, she turned and continued on her way, her steps carrying her towards an uncertain destiny.

Delia's internal alert went off. She sensed more than saw the threat, but she knew it was real. The sound of a stick snapping behind the bushes that lined the river activated her killer instincts.

She knew her boss at the Organization was not happy with her progress, but would they have sent a team to take her out before she had a chance to complete the assignment? He had given her forty-eight hours, and the time was not up yet.

Having left her pistol at the apartment before leaving for Thorne's penthouse, she felt naked. She slid her hand under her skirt and pulled the knife from her thigh sheath.

She scanned the area, identifying threats from multiple locations still hidden in the trees. Delia's senses heightened. The prospect of facing a team of assassins sent by her own organization was daunting. With a mind sharpened by years of training, she assessed the situation.

She was outnumbered and outgunned, but her skills were not to be underestimated. With a swift movement, she ducked behind a large oak tree, using the shadows as her ally. She removed her high heels and stood, waiting for the chance to make her first move.

The moonlight provided her with just enough visibility to navigate the terrain. She moved from tree to tree with the stealth she'd developed over her years of experience. She could make out three figures, their silhouettes menacing against the night sky. Their steps were methodical, closing in on her position.

Delia's breath slowed, as did her pulse, and her gaze remained steady. She knew her life as an assassin had prepared her for moments like these, but her decision to turn away from her mission added a layer of complexity.

Delia recognized the telltale signs of professional killers, their bodies coiled and ready to strike. In that moment, she felt a surge of adrenaline, her instincts taking over. She waited until one assassin was within striking distance. With a graceful movement, she stepped out from her hiding place, her knife dull in the moonlight.

The closest assassin raised his pistol towards the threat that appeared like an apparition out of nowhere, but he was a second too late, and the knife sliced into his throat like a scalpel. He gurgled as blood erupted from his throat, and Delia grabbed his wrist, kicked out the back of his knee and dropped him to the ground. She pulled him behind the tree and relieved him of his weapon.

The other figures paused, their forms becoming more distinct. They moved into the trees on the opposite side of the sidewalk from the river and spread out. The battle had begun, and Delia's skills would be put to the test. Each move was intentional, each strike precise, as she fought for her life. The night echoed with the rustle of leaves, a deadly battle unfolding by the river's edge.

Delia's heart pounded as she assessed her new advantage. The pistol, now in her hand, offered a glimmer of hope. She knew her attackers would not relent; they were persistent shadows, lurking in the night.

With careful movements, she stepped farther into the cover of the trees, her back to the river. The moonlight, once her ally, now cast an eerie glow on the scene, illuminating the shadows and light. She could sense their presence, their movements, like dark spirits, closing in. This was her domain, the realm of the assassin, and she would not go down without a fight.

A rustle of leaves signaled the closest attacker's position. Delia's knife flashed in the moonlight as she threw it with deadly accuracy. The blade found its mark, and the figure stumbled, a dark shadow collapsing among the trees. She moved to his position and found him lying on the dirt, the blade sticking out of his throat just above his ballistic vest. She wasted no time and shot him once in the head with the silenced pistol and pulled the knife from his throat, wiping the blood on his sleeve. Silence followed, thick with anticipation.

She knew the remaining assassin would be more cautious now, their prey proving more formidable than expected. The soft hum of the city seemed distant, the night enveloping them in an isolating embrace. Every muscle in Delia's body was tense and ready. She felt a strange sense of empowerment in this game of life and death, her survival instincts taking over. With a swift movement, she darted to the side, using the trees as cover. The attacker responded, his steps precise, trying to predict her next move. But Delia had the advantage of knowing the terrain. She had walked this path many times over the years, and now her life depended on outmaneuvering the shadows.

The river was a silent witness, its soft murmur a stark contrast to the violence unfolding on its banks. As Delia moved, her mind raced, strategizing her next steps. She knew her skills were being tested, but she knew she would prevail.

Delia's heart raced as she awaited the remaining assassin's next move. Her mind, sharpened by years of training and experience, worked to formulate a strategy. She knew her decision to betray her mission and spare Thorne would put a target on her back, and now she found herself facing the consequences of her decision.

She could sense the assassin's presence, feel his eyes on her, but his form was hidden by the shadows. A rustle of leaves gave away the attacker's position, and Delia reacted. She fired a shot in his direction, the bullet slicing through the air. The figure stumbled, and she dashed to a new hiding spot, using the trees as cover.

The assassin, undeterred, continued his pursuit, his steps deliberate and purposeful. Delia's breath quickened as she moved.

Delia stayed low, listening to the sounds of the night. She knew her assassin was close but didn't realize how close until he passed on the other side of the tree she kneeled behind. She stepped around the tree as he passed, and she raised the pistol.

The assassin stopped. He knew she was behind him, but he had no choice. He dove to the side, firing a shot from under his arm as he dove, then he hit the ground, rolled and jumped to his feet. The bullet slammed into his head, and he fell back into the bushes.

Delia approached the body and checked him for a radio or any identification, not that she expected to find either. The Organization was too good at this to make that kind of mistake.

She stepped onto the sidewalk, looked around and, seeing no one near, pulled each body from the woods and removed their weapons and ammunition. She shoved them into the river, and they sank out of sight.

She placed her knife back in the sheath on her thigh, found her shoes where she'd left them and raced barefoot into the night. She needed to get back to Thorne's penthouse.

| 16 |

The Attempted Rescue

Delia's heart was pounding as she raced through the night, the cool air whipping against her face. The adrenaline coursing through her veins gave her a sense of heightened awareness, and she felt more alive than ever.

She knew she had made the right choice in sparing Thorne, even if it meant becoming a target herself. The thought of him waiting for her at his penthouse, unaware of the danger she had just faced, brought a surge of protectiveness to her. She had to get back to him to ensure his safety.

As she navigated the city streets, her mind retraced the steps that had led her to this moment. The kiss, the art gallery, her internal struggle—it all felt like a blur. Now, more than ever, she was determined to leave her life as an assassin behind. Thorne had shown her a glimpse of a different existence, and she was willing to risk everything for a chance at redemption.

The Organization she had once served felt like a shackle she was ready to break free from. But first, she had to ensure Thorne's safety and confront the dangers that lay ahead.

The night seemed to stretch endlessly as Delia made her way back to Thorne's penthouse. With each step, she felt a growing sense of purpose and resolve. As she approached the penthouse, lit by the moon's glow, she felt a sense of hope amidst the uncertainty.

Delia pushed open the glass doors and stepped into the lobby, her pistol moving from side to side. There were no security guards at the reception desk, and her senses heightened.

Leading with her pistol, she stepped around the counter. The security guard, an older man with gray hair and a potbelly, lay slumped on the floor in a pool of blood. The front of his white shirt was covered in blood, and his eyes were open with shock. Delia's breath caught in her throat as she took in the gruesome scene. The absence of the security guard at his post had been unnerving, but finding him lying in a pool of his own blood sent a chill down her spine.

She knew that her decision to spare Thorne had put her on a collision course with her former organization, and now the consequences were laid bare before her. Every instinct screamed at her to flee, to put as much distance as possible between herself and this place of danger. But she couldn't leave Thorne unprotected.

She kneeled beside the guard, feeling for a pulse despite knowing it was futile. The Organization had moved quickly, and she knew they wouldn't stop until Thorne was dead and she was dead or back under their control. She had to get to Thorne, to warn him and formulate a plan. Her heart pounded with a mixture of fear and determination as she rose to her feet, her eyes scanning the lobby for any further signs of intrusion.

Delia moved with purpose towards the elevator, her fingers tightening around the pistol. She knew that the next few moments could determine not just her future but also her very survival.

As the elevator doors slid open, Delia stepped inside, her gaze fixed on the buttons as if they held some hidden answer. With a steady hand, she selected the floor two below Thorne's penthouse, her mind racing through potential scenarios. Would she find Thorne unharmed, or would she walk into another scene of violence?

The elevator's smooth ascent felt agonizingly slow, each second stretching out like an eternity. Delia knew that once those doors opened again, there was no turning back. She was committed to this path, and whatever lay ahead, she would face it head-on, driven by her newfound desire for redemption.

The elevator doors opened, and she stepped through, her senses on high alert. She moved down the hall towards the fire stairs, stopped and placed her ear against the door. Hearing nothing on the other side, she pushed the door open and slipped through, expecting a shot to come out of nowhere. The shot never came.

Delia made her way up the stairs to the penthouse door and paused. She held the pistol ready and opened the door, stepping through and crouching low. She spotted the body of a housekeeper lying next to the elevator door. She had been shot once in the back and once in the back of the head.

Delia placed her high heels next to the stairwell door, raised her pistol and walked towards the main living area.

Delia's heart hammered in her chest as she stepped farther the penthouse, her pistol raised and her eyes scanning the familiar surroundings for any signs of intrusion. The elegant furnishings and expensive artwork now took on a sinister air, each shadow a potential hiding place for an unseen threat.

She moved with purpose, her footsteps soft and steady. The silence was oppressive, and she held her breath, straining to hear any telltale sounds that would indicate Thorne's presence, or that of an intruder.

As she approached the master bedroom, her hand tightened around the pistol, her finger hovering over the trigger. The door had been destroyed; she pushed open what remained, ready for whatever she encountered. The room was empty. Other than the damaged door, there were no signs of a struggle, no sign that Thorne had ever been there. But there was something in the air. A lingering smell of jasmine. She hadn't noticed it before. She knew that smell from her past, but there was no way. That part of her life had ended in tragedy a long time ago. She shook off the thoughts and moved on.

A chill ran down Delia's spine as she realized the implications. Could Thorne have been taken? The Organization had moved swiftly and efficiently, but had they moved that quickly? Were the assassins she encountered along the river a diversion?

She knew their methods well, having employed them herself on countless occasions. A wave of nausea washed over her as she imagined Thorne in their hands, vulnerable and unaware of the danger he faced. She had to find him, and fast. Every second that ticked by increased the likelihood of him coming to harm.

With renewed determination, Delia turned to leave the bedroom. She felt a surge of anger and protectiveness, fueling her determination to get him back. With a deep breath, she steadied herself, knowing that she needed to stay focused and rely on her training. Her desire for redemption would have to be her anchor in the storm that was sure to come.

As she turned to leave the bedroom, her gaze fell on the moonlit cityscape beyond the window, and she knew that her life as an assassin was behind her. This was her path now, and she would face whatever came next with courage and resolve.

With her pistol raised, she continued her search, her eyes darting across the room for any clues that could lead her to Thorne. The silence was deafening, and the coldness of the penthouse felt like a trap, each corner hiding a potential threat.

Delia's heart pounded as she moved with calculated steps. She understood her former employer's determination to secure what they desired was absolute.

As she reached the kitchen, the sight that greeted her made her stomach drop. The body of the chef who had prepared their meals with such care now lay slumped across the counter, a knife protruding from his back. The absence of any sign of a struggle indicated he had been taken by surprise.

Delia's mind raced as she tried to make sense of the scene before her. The Organization had sent a message, but what were they trying to tell her? Were they asserting their dominance, or was this a warning of what was to come?

As she stood there, a sense of determination washed over her. She would not let them win. She had visualized a life beyond the shadows, and she was willing to fight for it.

She continued her search of the penthouse and then stopped by the living room windows overlooking the city. The housekeeper and chef were dead, but there were no dead or injured security officers in the rest of the penthouse. She had read the dossiers on Thorne's security staff and knew they were men and women of integrity. They would never have abandoned him. A thought slipped into her consciousness. Was it possible that Thorne and his team had escaped before the blitz attack that had claimed the lives of his staff?

Delia's mind raced as she processed this new information. The absence of security officers among the casualties and Thorne's apparent disappearance suggested a well-coordinated escape. But where could he have gone?

Her thoughts turned to the other safe locations she was aware of. They were the most obvious choices, but would he have taken the risk of leading his captors to those havens?

A sense of urgency washed over her as she realized that time was of the essence. The Organization would not rest until they found Thorne, and every second that passed increased the danger he faced.

Delia's heart pounded as she left the penthouse, her mind racing with potential leads and strategies. As she descended the stairs, her footsteps echoing in the empty stairwell, she felt compassion for Thorne and a deep-seated need to keep him safe. She would use all the resources at her disposal to find him and, in doing so, sever her ties with her past as an assassin.

Delia stopped on the ground floor, and a thought crept into her psyche. What about David? With all that had gone on, she had forgotten about her husband, and a fresh fear overtook her. Would the Organization go after David to get to her? She knew the director was ruthless, but David was an innocent.

She wiped the pistol off on her skirt and dropped it into the trash can at the elevator landing. She stepped behind the reception desk, picked up a piece of paper and a pen, wrote the word "penthouse" on it and placed it next to the phone. She pushed the button on the phone console, waited for the dial tone and dialed 911.

She stepped around the counter and walked out of the building as the voice of the emergency operator came on the line. She needed to get home to David. Her emotions were raw, and she needed to make sure he was safe; she needed something from him she knew she could depend on. Then she would turn her efforts to finding a man who was difficult to find in the best of times.

| 17 |

A New Player

The elevator doors swallowed Delia, the metallic clang echoing Thorne's frantic heartbeat. He could have called her back, reeled her in with a single word. He remembered the electric thrum of their kiss, the raw, desperate hunger she'd tried to conceal. But he wouldn't. Let her chase him. Let her earn him. He wouldn't cheapen it.

The city lights, a million glittering daggers plunged into the black velvet night, blurred through his expansive window. His reflection stared back at him—a haunted landscape etched with sleepless nights, a face sculpted by a lifetime of controlled fury now cracked open, revealing the raw, bleeding vulnerability beneath.

A shadow separated itself from the gloom, a predator materializing in the periphery. He turned. The scent of her expensive jasmine perfume filled the air.

"You want her, Thorne," she purred, a slow, predatory smile twisting her lips. "I felt it in the vault—the raw animal heat between you. Something stopped her, something . . . cold."

He swirled the amber liquid in his glass, the ice clinking like a death knell.

"Caution," he said. "Apparently, my legendary charm failed to impress her enough to sleep with me." He smiled.

Delia was beautiful, but sleeping with her was a means to an end, a conquest to be heralded. He felt he had won her over. He just needed to keep playing the game.

The words hung on his tongue, laced with the bitter metallic tang of betrayal. He offered her a drink, a gesture as cold and precise as a surgeon's incision. She refused, her blue eyes—pools of shimmering venom—fixed on him. The crimson fire of her hair cascaded down her back, framing a face of exquisite porcelain, a mask hiding a killer's heart.

Her blouse strained against the swell of her breasts, a blatant invitation beneath the tailored suit. Her legs, a breathtaking length beneath the hem of her skirt, were sculpted limbs ready to spring. He sat opposite her, the silence thick with unspoken threats.

A snap of her fingers summoned a silent guard, a grim shadow who deposited a manila folder in her hand before melting back into the shadows. She opened it, her smile widening into a chilling grimace.

She tossed him the file. The paper felt brittle and cold against his fingers. He scanned the report, the blood draining from his face.

"You never told me she was an assassin. You told me she was after the files—a thief, not a . . . a contract killer." He stared at her, the world tilting on its axis. The cold realization hit him like a physical blow. The files were an extra, had she retrieved them." The words were choked, raw with the terrifying clarity of impending death.

Thorne picked up his glass and swallowed his drink, walked to the bar and poured a new one, larger than the first.

"Who the fuck hired her?" he asked, swallowing the drink.

"Someone who wants to stop you from selling your app," she said. "Chinese, Russians, our own people. Could be anyone."

"But I wasn't planning on selling it. My app will help people. It needs to be shared."

She looked at him like he had two heads. "Your app is a weapon, and we will make billions selling it to my client."

"It was never meant to be this way," he said, his voice raspy with exhaustion. His gaze met hers, a plea for understanding in his eyes. "I wanted to connect the world, to break down barriers, not create them."

She stood up, walked over and wrapped her arms around him. "Your app can be used for good," she said. "Think of all the good you can do with all that money. All the people you can help."

"I won't be able to do shit if I'm dead."

He reached out, his hand trembling, and gestured towards the vast expanse of the city before them.

"Look at it," he said, his voice hoarse. "All that potential, all those lives . . . and I have the power to control them. But the responsibility . . . it's crushing. Can we find out who she is working for?" he asked.

"We probably can," she said. "Then what? Our plan, since we found out about her, was to use her as a conduit to mislead the wrong people and encourage the right ones. That doesn't change because she kills people for a living. We need to bring her over to our side. Then we can use her to eliminate some of the competition and, as a result, drive the price higher."

He turned and wrapped his arms around her. Thorne's mind raced, the alcohol doing little to dull the sharp edges of his panic.

"We need to find her, turn her or . . ." His voice trailed off, the unspoken alternative hanging heavy in the air.

"Or what?" she challenged, her eyes narrowing. "You'd have me kill her? The woman who might just save your life?"

Thorne's gaze dropped to the folder, his jaw clenching. "I don't want anyone else to die because of me." He ran a hand through his hair, the gesture one of frustration and defeat. "I just want this to be over."

A soft laugh escaped her, a sound devoid of humor. "It's never over, Thorne. It's the nature of our business. There will always be another threat, another assassin. Embrace it." Her eyes glittered with a feverish intensity. "Use Delia. Turn her into a weapon for us."

Thorne shook his head, his voice tight. "I won't use her like that. I won't be responsible for more blood on my hands."

"Then wash your hands of it," she snapped. "Let me handle this. It's what I do, remember? Clean up your messes, protect your interests."

Thorne's silence was his consent. She knew it, and a satisfied smile curved her lips. "Consider it done," she murmured, her voice once again the silken purr of a predator.

Thorne's mind raced, the wheels turning in his head as he grappled with the revelation. Delia was an assassin sent to kill him. The very thought sent a chill down his spine. And yet, there was something intriguing about it all. He knew the game they played, the delicate movement of shadows and secrets. But this . . . this was different. This was personal.

"We need to find her," he said, his voice steady despite the turmoil within him. "But how?"

The woman, a serpentine seductress, smiled, her jade eyes glinting with a cunning light. "We use what we have. Information is power, and we have something she wants."

Thorne's eyes narrowed, understanding dawning. "The files. She came for the files, but I told her they were fake. She knows I have the real files."

A slow, predatory grin spread across the woman's face, her lips curving in a mirror of Thorne's own dangerous smile. "Exactly. We dangle the files as bait, and she'll come running. It's a hunter's game, Thorne. Let's see if this angel can fly."

Thorne's look grew intense as he contemplated the trap they would set. "And if she's working for our people?"

The woman's smile never wavered. "Then we'll know soon enough. But mark my words, Thorne, Delia is a wild card, an unpredictable force. We use that to our advantage, and we just might survive."

She kissed him hard on the lips, her mouth probing his. He could feel her breast swell with anticipation. He felt her heat rise, and he pulled her closer. He broke the embrace, took her hand and turned towards the hall leading to the master bedroom.

"Sir," said a voice behind him.

He turned to see his lead security guard approaching. "What is it, Frank?" Four other security guards were coming into the room, all with weapons drawn.

"Sir, we have intruders in the lobby. We need to get you out of here."

Thorne looked at Frank. "What do you mean, intruders?"

"Not sure, sir. We need to move. Now!"

Intruders? His gaze flicked to the woman, a silent question passing between them. She gave an almost imperceptible nod, her eyes narrowing.

"It could be a diversion," she murmured. "A tactic to split our forces, expose vulnerabilities."

Thorne's jaw clenched. "Or it could be Delia, coming for me."

He turned to Frank, his voice sharp with command. "How many intruders? And where is Delia?"

Frank's face was grim. "We don't know, sir. We've lost contact with the lobby team. As for Delia, we haven't seen her since she left the building."

Thorne's heart hammered in his chest.

"We need to move," Frank urged. "Now."

Thorne glanced at the woman, his eyes flicking to the folder still clutched in his hand. He looked at Frank.

"We need to get to the mansion. I need to secure the app files."

Frank nodded, and they moved down the hall towards the master bedroom. He pushed a button on the nightstand console. The bedroom door shut and latched. A second button opened the door to the stairwell that led to the roof.

The helicopter's blades were already turning as they raced across the roof and jumped into the chopper. The pilot wasted no time, and as soon as they were in and the doors closed, they were airborne. Thorne's mind raced as the helicopter soared over the city. The woman, a mysterious and deadly enigma, sat beside him, her eyes fixed on the sprawling metropolis below.

"We need to find Delia before she finds you," she said, her voice sharp with urgency. "She's a skilled hunter, and she knows you have the files. We can't underestimate her."

Thorne's gaze darkened as he considered the assassin's motivations. "Why me? Why send her after me?" he asked, his voice tight with a mixture of fear and anger. "What's in my app that's worth killing for? Even if I'm dead, the app will still be released, but then it will be released as open source and available to anyone. My adversaries would be foolish to do that."

The woman's eyes narrowed, her face a mask of determination. "Your app is a game changer, Thorne. It's a digital key that can unlock any door, bypass any security measure. With it, someone could access government secrets or corporate intelligence, or even manipulate public opinion on a global scale. It's a weapon, and whoever controls it holds the power."

Thorne's heart pounded in his chest as the implications sank in. "So, it's not just my life at stake," he realized. "It's the security of the entire world."

The woman's jade eyes glittered in the dim light of the helicopter. "And that's why we must find Delia. We need to know who she's working for and what their intentions are. In the wrong hands, your creation could bring nations to their knees."

Thorne nodded, his jaw set in a resolute line. "Then we set the trap. Use the files as bait."

The helicopter descended towards the mansion, a beacon of wealth and power amidst the sprawling city. Thorne's mind raced with strategies, his fear fueling his determination to protect his creation and the world.

| 18 |

A Need for Clarity

Delia's heart pounded as she raced down the long, winding road. She could feel the weight bearing down on her as she thought about the danger that awaited her. She knew she was putting herself at risk by defying the Organization, but she couldn't just sit idly by if they targeted her husband. David was her everything, and she would do anything to protect him.

Had they been watching her, waiting for the perfect moment to strike? She felt a surge of anger at the thought of being constantly monitored by the Organization, but she pushed it aside. There was no time for anger or regret. She had to focus on getting to David before it was too late.

As she drove, the city lights faded behind her, and the darkness of the countryside surrounded her. The endless miles of empty road seemed to stretch on forever, but Delia refused to let fear consume her. She was determined to reach David and warn him of the danger that was coming his way. She couldn't bear the thought of losing him, and she knew he would do everything in his power to keep her safe. They were a team, and they would face this threat together.

With each passing mile, she could feel her determination growing stronger. She would do whatever it took to protect her loved ones, and she refused to let the Organization win.

Delia's hands tightened on the steering wheel as she thought about the secrets and lies she had unwittingly become entangled in. The Organization's reach seemed infinite, and their methods were ruthless. She knew that going against them was akin to signing her own death warrant, but the thought of David in their crosshairs fueled her with a courage she didn't know she possessed.

The night enveloped her like a cloak, shielding her from prying eyes. She imagined the Organization's agents scouring the city for her, their frustration growing as they realized she had given them the slip. A small smile played on her lips at the thought. They had underestimated her, assuming she would accept their threats. But Delia was made of stronger stuff, and her love for David gave her a strength they could never expect.

As the city became a distant memory, Delia allowed herself a moment of reflection. She thought of the life she and David had built, the dreams they shared and the future they had envisioned. It was a future worth fighting for, worth risking everything for. With each revolution of the wheels, she drew closer to David, and the prospect of seeing him again gave her the strength to face whatever lay ahead.

She parked her SUV around the corner from her house and made her way through the trees and bushes of the adjoining neighbors' houses. She moved like the wind. Reaching the edge of the backyard, she sat for a few minutes in the dark, her eyes scanning her house. There were no lights on inside. She checked her watch. It was late enough that David was probably already asleep.

She moved across the backyard and stopped at the back door to the kitchen. She unlocked the door and slipped inside. Her heart hammered in her chest as she stepped into the kitchen, her eyes scanning the familiar surroundings for any sign of intrusion. The moonlight filtering through the window provided soft illumination, casting an eerie glow on the counters and floors.

She moved with purpose, her footsteps soft and measured as she made her way towards the staircase. She listened for any sound or movement that might indicate an intruder. As she reached the bottom step, she paused, listening for any hint of disturbance in the house. The silence stretched, thick with anticipation.

With a steady hand, she reached for the railing and began her ascent, her eyes fixed on the upper landing. At the top of the stairs, she found herself in the hallway leading to their bedroom. Delia's breath caught in her throat as she approached the door. She pushed it open, her heart in her throat. She heard David breathing, and she let out a sigh of relief.

She backed out of the room and stepped into the guest bathroom across the hall. She stripped off her dirty and bloody clothes and climbed into the shower, the hot water feeling good against her skin. She rinsed off, turned off the water and slipped out of the shower.

Her mind wandered as she dried herself. She thought of the kiss in the art vault and the sudden, reckless emotion that had accompanied it. Her body tingled, and she knew what she needed. She stepped out of the bathroom and walked into her bedroom. She slipped under the covers and listened to David breathe. Unable to wait any longer, she slid her hand under the covers and felt for David. She could feel him respond, and he moaned as he woke, pushed her onto her back and rolled on top of her. He slid into her, and she moaned and wrapped herself around him. She knew she was where she belonged.

Her body satisfied, she looked at David. He smiled at her. "What happened with your client? You were a wild woman tonight, so your client must have driven you crazy."

Delia smiled. "You know billionaires. We had to arrive at a settlement, and you would have thought we were taking his entire fortune away from him. By the time we were finished drafting the details, he had already made back all the money we were offering. Listening to him whine drove me crazy."

Her body tingled, and it took her a moment to realize that while she spoke, David had been tracing circles with his finger around her nipples. She felt an explosion coming on, so she pushed him flat, straddled him and guided him inside her. She screamed into his shoulder.

***

Shafts of sunlight streamed through the blinds on the patio door, painting stripes across Delia's eyelids. She blinked, the warmth of the blankets a comforting weight. David's side of the king-sized bed, a rumpled landscape of blankets and pillows was empty. She traced the faint indentation of his shoulder in the pillow, the memory of his warmth a pressure against her fingertips. A sigh escaped her lips, a sound lost in the quiet hum of the air conditioner.

Then, a low thrumming started deep inside her—a residual heat, a lingering echo of his touch. Her fingers drifted lower, exploring the still-sensitive skin of her thighs. A slow smile curved her lips as she recalled the whispered promises, the rough-spun sheets tangled between their bodies. She closed her eyes, letting the wave of sensation wash over her, a tide pulling her under. When she opened her eyes, the sunlight had shifted, painting the bedroom in a different hue. She lay back, limbs heavy with a pleasant exhaustion, a faint sheen of perspiration on her brow. A slow, contented smile played on her lips—a smile that spoke volumes. The quiet purr of the air conditioner was the counterpoint to the silent symphony playing within her.

By the time she reached the kitchen, David had already left for work. She put on a pair of shorts, a T-shirt and her running shoes and ran through the neighborhood. All was secure, and she saw no sign of any imminent threat. She returned home and stepped into her office. She knew David rarely set the alarm system if he was home alone, so she activated all the exterior cameras and set them to run continuously and to trigger an alarm on her phone if a prowler was picked up. Since they were not connected to the home power supply, they would be difficult to shut down without getting to the source. For the moment, she felt David would be safe. She needed to prepare for what came next with Thorne, but first she had something to take care of.

| 19 |

Small Revenge

Delia had spent the morning running a background check on the name she had received from the director, and she was surprised by what she found. Beverly Cooper had been Robert Masters's partner in the firm of Masters and Cooper Capital since day one. They had been friends in college and had left their jobs at a mergers and acquisitions firm to start their own hedge fund. They were hugely successful, but there was trouble on the horizon.

Beverly Cooper was being investigated by the SEC and the Department of Justice for fraud and embezzlement. The secret investigation was ongoing, and according to the information she could find using all the vast resources of the Organization, Robert Masters was cooperating in the investigation and was not suspected of any wrongdoing. She couldn't determine how Beverly Cooper had discovered the investigation, but somehow she did. After reading everything she found, she had come to one conclusion: Beverly Cooper, with the help of an asset in an unnamed government agency, had used the Organization to take out a hit on Robert Masters.

Delia was pissed. She had taken a good man's life on faulty information, but she was going to make this right. Delia, dressed in jeans and a T-shirt, slipped her knife into a sheath at the back of her jeans and removed her pistol from the nightstand. She opened the garage door, slid into her SUV and pulled down the driveway. There was a fury burning in her that she was going to put out the only way she knew how.

She parked in front of Beverly Cooper's townhouse and waited for dark. Clouds had hidden the moon, so other than a few ornamental streetlights, placed more for ambiance than light, the area around the complex was dark.

Beverly Cooper pulled her Mercedes down the narrow driveway and pulled into the two-car garage that belonged to the end unit. She closed the door and entered the townhouse. Delia checked her knife and her pistol and exited her SUV. She strolled casually along the sidewalk, passing by Cooper's unit twice. She noticed a light come on in what she assumed was an upstairs bedroom, and she looked around and approached the front door.

Acting like she was waiting for someone to answer, Delia used her lockpicks to unlock the door and slipped inside. The alarm panel hung dark on the wall, which Delia hated. She had a problem with women who had the means to protect themselves at their disposal and didn't use them. She checked the ground floor to make sure Beverly didn't have any guests over and took a seat at the kitchen table. There was an open bottle of wine on the table and a couple of glasses on the credenza behind the table, so Delia poured herself a drink and waited, her pistol sitting on the table.

Beverly Cooper, dressed in sweats and barefoot, strolled into the kitchen and turned on the light. Delia took a sip of wine and set the glass on the table, hard enough to just barely be heard. Cooper turned with a start. She was holding a small steak knife in her hand.

Delia smiled and raised the pistol.

"What do you want?" asked Cooper, hiding her surprise and attempting to sound in control.

"What I want, Beverly, is to find out why you took out a contract on your partner, Robert."

Cooper's face paled. "Robert was stealing from the company, and I couldn't get anyone to listen."

"So you decided the best way to handle it was to have him killed. Seems rather extreme," said Delia.

Cooper slid one foot towards the door, and Delia laughed. "Beverly, please don't move. I don't care how fast you think you are, you won't beat the bullet. So move back towards the sink and put the knife down. That's not going to help you. Now, we both know that Robert was working with the Feds to build a case against you. Don't bother denying it. I have all the documents, and they are compelling. Somehow, you found out about the grand jury and the upcoming indictment and decided to eliminate the one witness against you." Delia stopped for a second for effect.

"Robert Masters was a decent man who was working on being a better father to his three young boys, who, thanks to you, are now fatherless. So here's what we are going to do."

Delia pointed to the briefcase sitting on the counter. "Please pull out your laptop and open your personal bank account."

Cooper's hands shook as she pulled out the laptop and opened it.

"You won't get away with this. I can make your life miserable," said Cooper, her voice cracking.

Delia laughed. "Open your banking app." Delia's voice was as cold as ice.

Cooper opened the app and stood to the side. "So you're going to rob me? Is that your plan? I don't know who you are, but I have lots of friends in very high places. Your life won't be worth shit when I get done with you." Sweat formed on her forehead.

"No, Beverly. I'm not going to rob you. I'm going to collect on a contract."

"What contract?" asked Cooper.

Delia smiled. "Why, the contract you took out on yourself."

Delia pulled the trigger, and a small hole appeared in Cooper's forehead. She crashed back into the sink, and Delia caught her before she hit the floor and lowered her gently to the tile. She took the laptop to the kitchen table and sat. She pulled out her phone, opened a different banking app and pulled up an account that had been opened a few hours ago. It was a custodial account in the name of the Masters children. She set up a transfer from Cooper's account to the children's account and transferred everything out of Cooper's various accounts. The amount totaled fourteen million dollars. She was certain that Cooper had other accounts, but this would do for now.

Delia closed the banking apps and pulled up an anonymous, untraceable email account. She opened a new email and emailed the children's mother. She typed in the account and bank information and hit send. She closed the laptop, walked to the sink and washed her wineglass, leaving Beverly Cooper lying on the floor. She felt better about herself. She knew from experience what it was like to lose a parent at such a young age, but she hoped the money would help. Delia headed back home.

| 20 |

A Web of Intrigue

The club was a gathering place for men of power and influence, and it was the perfect venue from which the director could spin his webs of intrigue—those life-and death decisions that kept the Organization busy. But tonight, the mahogany tables gleamed with a sinister reflection of his own turmoil.

The director sat in a high-backed leather armchair; the brandy burned a path down his throat, a stark contrast to the icy dread clenching his heart. The crystal glass was a fragile symbol of the composure the director himself lacked. His guest sat opposite him.

"What happened to the team we sent after Delia?" he asked, his voice rougher than its usual controlled baritone.

He took another sip, the brandy doing little to soothe the churning in his stomach.

"I think we have to assume they will not be returning to the office," said his guest, his tone measured. "That was a waste of good talent. You knew she wouldn't go down without a fight."

The words hung in the air, a damning indictment. The director did know this, and an icy knot of guilt twisted in his gut. He'd sent them, hadn't he? His own hand had signed their death warrants, though he'd hidden behind the euphemism of neutralizing assets. Delia was more than an asset; she was . . . almost family. The thought sent a fresh wave of nausea through him. He'd sacrificed his morals for the Organization, a price he'd rationalized for years, but now the cost felt too high.

"We needed to do something," he mumbled. "She hasn't fulfilled her contract, and I have no idea what's going on in that beautiful head of hers. Has she fallen for this Thorne?" The question felt pathetic, desperate, a weak attempt to justify his actions.

The guest sipped his water. "She has never not fulfilled a mission. We needed to give her the benefit of the doubt. Instead, you sent a hit team after her, putting her on alert. Has she tried to reach out?"

"No," the director said, his voice tight with a mixture of anger and despair. "She's been off the grid for over twenty-four hours."

The silence stretched, filled with the clinking of ice in his glass—a brittle sound that mirrored the shattering of his composure. He'd failed. He'd failed Delia, he'd failed the Organization, and most important, he'd failed his clients.

His guest frowned. He knew Delia was the consummate professional, but the director's frantic energy, his palpable fear, was unnerving. It spoke of something more profound than a simple mission gone awry.

"Has the team you sent after Thorne checked in?" the guest asked, his voice sharper now, sensing the director's unraveling.

"Yes," the director said, the words tasting like ash in his mouth. "Thorne wasn't at the penthouse. There was . . . collateral damage. The team took out a security guard, a housekeeper and Thorne's personal chef. I sent them on to the mansion, hoping he might turn up there. They're still at the mansion, waiting."

He paused, the brandy doing nothing to numb the growing sense of dread.

"Thorne has been hiding for years. He could be anywhere," he said.

He knew, with a chilling certainty, that he'd made a mistake. The collateral damage wasn't accidental; it was a sign of his own escalating desperation, a violent lashing out fueled by fear and regret. He'd chosen violence against one of his own, a path he knew was wrong, and now he was trapped in the consequences, the cold certainty of his own failure settling upon him like a shroud.

The guest set down his glass, the movement deliberate and calm, a stark contrast to the director's mounting anxiety.

"We must consider the possibility that Delia and Thorne are working together. If she has gone rogue, it is a concern, but it changes nothing. We find her, we bring her in and we deal with Thorne."

The director's eyes narrowed, the brandy clouding his thoughts with a hazy fury. "What if she doesn't want to be found? What if she's chosen him over us?"

The guest's expression remained impassive, but his eyes held a hint of pity. "Then we have our answer. She has become a liability, and we treat her as such. It is a risk we take with every agent, and you know it well. Sometimes, people cannot be controlled, no matter how tightly we try to hold the reins."

The director's knuckles turned white as he gripped the armrests, the leather creaking under the strain. "I will not accept that. Not from her. She owes her life to this organization, to me. I pulled her from the streets, gave her a purpose, and this is how she repays me?" His voice rose, the brandy-fueled anger spilling over. "Find her," he growled. "And bring her back. By any means necessary." The guest nodded, his face a mask of composure, but his eyes held a warning. "As you wish. But remember, Director, the tighter you try to hold the sand, the faster it slips through your fingers."

The director waved him off, his mind already spinning with the next move. He would not let Delia go. She would be found, and she would pay for her betrayal.

The guest rose, his movements graceful and unhurried, a stark contrast to the director's pent-up tension. He knew better than to linger, sensing the storm brewing within his superior. As he turned to leave, the director's voice, thick with power and position, boomed, "I want updates, and I want them frequently."

The guest nodded, his face a study in calm obedience, but his eyes, cold and calculating, held a world of unspoken thoughts. When the door closed behind him, the director was alone with his thoughts, the silence a heavy weight in the opulent room. He poured himself another brandy from the decanter on the small table, his hand steadying as he considered his next move. Delia and Thorne, a dangerous combination, were now his primary targets. He knew the game had changed, and the hunters had become the hunted.

The director's mind, a strategic battlefield, plotted and planned. He saw Delia, her face a blur of loyalty and betrayal, and Thorne, a shadow lurking in the corners of his vision. They were a threat, a loose end that needed to be tied, and the director would use every resource at his disposal to find them. He knew their strengths, their weaknesses, and he would exploit them without mercy.

He sipped his brandy and nodded to several other members as they walked by, heading for the dining room or the bar. He looked up and spotted his guest walking back towards him, his expression grave.

"I have an update, sir. It seems our agents have located Thorne, or at least, they've found his trail."

The director shifted in his seat, his brandy forgotten, his eyes gleaming with a dangerous light. "Go on," he urged, his voice low and dangerous.

The guest's eyes narrowed, and he leaned in, his voice a hushed whisper. "They've picked up activity at one of his old safe houses. It's possible he's lying low there, but we can't be certain. It could be a trap, or a red herring."

The director's mind raced, his eyes fixed on the crystal glass in his hand, the brandy forgotten. "Send a team to investigate. I want eyes on the location, but no engagement unless they're certain Thorne is there. We don't want a repeat of the last fiasco." His voice was steady now, the alcohol-fueled anger replaced by a cold, deliberate determination. "And Delia?" he asked, his eyes lifting to meet his guest's. "Have there been any signs of her?"

The guest shook his head, his expression grim. "None, sir. But I have my people working on it. We'll find her, and when we do, we'll bring her back."

The director nodded, his eyes flicking to the other members of the club as they moved around them, oblivious to the dangerous game being played out in their midst. "See that you do," he said, his voice low and menacing. "And be discreet. I won't have the Organization or our client dragged through the mud before the deal is concluded. We have a lot riding on this."

The guest inclined his head, his face a mask of professionalism. "Understood, sir. Discretion is our top priority. We'll bring her in, and Thorne too, if he's still alive."

The director's lips twisted in a bitter smile. "Make sure you do, or don't come back yourself." It was a threat, and the guest knew it, but he nodded, turned and melted into the crowd, leaving the director alone with his dark thoughts.

The tuxedoed server, James, stepped up to the side of the chair. "Your dinner guest has arrived, your honor. I have shown her to your table. Shall I put your brandy back in the vault, or would you like it at your table?"

The director smiled, a thin veneer over the churning anxiety in his gut. He hadn't wanted this. Not this dinner, not this woman. He'd agreed, pressured by the whispers and threats from some of his clients. The promise of advancement, of ultimate power, was a tempting lure, dangling just out of reach. But the cost . . . the cost was Elena.

Elena, whose trusting eyes he'd betrayed with this charade. "That will be fine, James," he said, his voice tight. "We will have wine with dinner. Please bring a bottle of red and a bottle of white from my vault. I will leave the choice up to your excellent palate."

He stood, the polished wood of the chair cool against his trembling hand. This wasn't about power anymore; it was about a choice between his ambition and the woman he despised, a woman he would have killed as soon as their dealings were finished.

He knew this dinner was a terrible choice, a choice he would regret, but the clients she represented brought significant income to the Organization, and he couldn't just blow her off. He knew she was expecting an update on Thorne's Nexus app. He had made promises to several of his clients, and he was still far from being able to deliver. He hoped he could lie to her with a straight face.

He followed James with measured steps, but his heart pounded a frantic rhythm against his ribs—a drumbeat of his own moral collapse.

| 21 |

Lines Blurred

Delia showered, dressed in jeans and a black T-shirt and stepped into the kitchen. David had set the coffeepot to come on at the right time, and she sat down to a cup of hot coffee. She took the time to scramble a few eggs and some bacon, sat and enjoyed her breakfast while thinking about the past couple of days. After the night she and David had, she was convinced more than ever that he was her future.

She had feelings for Thorne. Not romantic feelings, but feelings she couldn't explain. She believed his decision to make his app available to the public for free was genuine, and she respected his morality. She thought about the fact that she had trashed her career to help Thorne, but she didn't regret the decision. She was tired of the double life she had been living, and she wanted a new start with her husband. She still felt obligated to protect Thorne from the Organization, but first she had to find him.

She was standing at the sink, washing the dishes, when she spotted movement in the trees behind the house. She assumed the Organization was watching her, but she needed to be free to find Thorne. She went up to her bedroom and opened the secret panel at the back of her closet. She strapped one of the composite knives to each leg, above her running shoes, chose her favorite 22-caliber pistol and threaded on the silencer. She closed the panel and left the bedroom.

She knew her SUV was parked around the corner, but she had to get to the trees without being seen. She decided the best approach was the most direct one. She stepped through the door into the garage and stood next to the door to the backyard. The door gave her the shortest distance to the tree line. She opened the door and ran for the trees. She didn't stop until she was deep enough into the trees that she had options to hide. She slipped behind an old oak, crouched low and held one knife in her hand.

The first pursuer moved through the trees, following the path he believed she had taken. He stepped past the old oak, and Delia struck from a crouch, driving the knife into his thigh. She pulled the knife out and drove it into his throat before he could yell. He fell to the ground, clutching his throat. She stepped past him and moved to her left. The second pursuer ran to his partner and kneeled next to him. Delia stepped from the bushes, placed the silencer against his head and pulled the trigger. He flopped onto the ground and died, never realizing what had happened. Delia headed for her SUV. She did not know if there were any other pursuers, but she needed to get moving.

Delia decided to start at the mansion by the sea. She knew that was one of Thorne's safe places, but she wasn't sure how safe it was with the Organization hot on his trail. She still wasn't certain if he was running or if the Organization had captured him at the penthouse, but she believed he was running. She also knew he would be surrounded by an army of security people. As she pulled away from the curb, her thoughts turned to Thorne.

As she spent time with him, she witnessed his unwavering dedication to his work and the genuine passion that burned within him. There was something about his vulnerability, his loneliness, that resonated with her, that chipped away at her hardened edges. She found herself drawn to him, not because of his wealth or influence, but because of the man beneath he wanted to be.

He was brilliant, yes, but also kind, empathetic. He spoke about his dream of a world free from war, a world where his technology could be used for good, and she saw a spark of hope in his eyes, a glimmer of something genuine that she had not encountered in years.

The thought of silencing him, of ending his life, no longer filled her with the detached professionalism she had once possessed. She saw the intensity of his focus, the unwavering drive that fueled his ambition. He was a force of nature, a whirlwind of energy and innovation, and she was swept up in his orbit, captivated by his brilliance.

She had seen a darkness in his eyes, a haunted look that hinted at a past filled with pain and regret. He had experienced the bitter fruit of success, had seen the darkness that lurked within humanity, and the weight of it pressed upon his soul. They were both survivors, both walking wounded, carrying the weight of their secrets.

| 22 |

Allies and Enemies

Delia drove with purpose, her mind focused on the task at hand. The mansion by the sea loomed in her thoughts, a potential sanctuary for Thorne, but also a trap if the Organization had beaten her there. She knew she had to be cautious, her movements deliberate. She knew the mansion was under surveillance.

As she neared the coast, the salty air whipped through the open windows of her SUV, carrying the familiar scent of the ocean. She followed the winding road, the trees giving way to expansive views of the rugged coastline.

The mansion came into view, perched atop a cliff, its grand architecture a stark contrast to the wild beauty of the sea. She parked her SUV out of sight and approached the mansion with caution. She knew from her conversation with Thorne that he had more cameras covering the property than she had realized. She needed to be extra careful. She knew making a daytime intrusion into his compound could be dangerous, but she needed to find him.

Aware of the danger her eyes scanned the surroundings for any sign of a trap. She spotted a place to get over the wall and moved like a spirit. She moved through the trees, avoiding several cameras and movement sensors. She stopped at the tree line and watched the mansion and the grounds. The place seemed deserted, but she knew looks could be deceiving.

She circled the building, looking for a way in. The last time she'd thought she had defeated the camera at the kitchen door, she found out that Thorne had a video of her entering.

She moved up onto the stone patio and located as many cameras as she could, hoping it would be enough. She moved to a window overlooking the patio and, using one of her knives, defeated the lock and slid it open. She climbed through and landed on the hardwood floor in a large butler's pantry. She pulled her pistol from her holster and, with the knife in her opposite hand, crept up to the door and listened.

The mansion was eerily quiet, the only sound the echo of her footsteps on the marble floors. She moved through the rooms, her heart pounding, half expecting to find Thorne or his captors around every corner.

She stepped into the hallway and found the first sign that she was too late. The bodies of two of Thorne's security guards lay in puddles of blood in the long hallway leading from the front door. She looked at the wounds on their torsos and throats. She now knew that the Organization was ahead of her.

As she made her way through the house, she found several more dead bodies. All security guards, and all dispatched in the same manner. It had been a blitz attack by people who were trained just like her. Delia's heart sank as she took in the grim scene. The bodies of Thorne's security detail, slain with ruthless efficiency, were a stark reminder of the danger that lay ahead.

She knew that the Organization had struck first, but she refused to turn back. Her determination to find Thorne, and perhaps even extract him from this perilous situation, burned within her. With her weapons at the ready, she continued her cautious progress through the mansion, every sense alert for any sign of movement or traps. The silence was unnerving, and she strained to hear any sound that might betray an enemy.

As she moved deeper into the heart of the mansion, she encountered more evidence of the violent struggle that had taken place. Bloodstains marred the elegant furnishings, and bullet holes punctured the walls. Thorne's captors had not expected the level of determination they had faced.

Despite the mounting signs of chaos and destruction, Delia maintained her focus. She knew that one wrong move could mean disaster, and so she proceeded with the utmost care, her eyes scanning for any advantage or hidden threat.

The silence was broken by the distant sound of footsteps and the faint murmur of voices. Delia froze, her body tensing as she assessed this recent development. She knew that her window of opportunity was narrowing.

With a steady hand, she readied her pistol, the metal cold against her palm. She took a steadying breath and moved forward, determined to find Thorne and offer him the sanctuary he needed.

The velvet curtain swallowed Delia whole. Two shadows, sleek as predators, glided past, their movements a blur of obsidian silk. Delia's emergence was a viper's strike. The silenced shots split the air and found their mark in the thighs of the man and woman. The ninja couple crumpled, the woman's strangled gasp echoing the man's muffled groan. The acrid bite of gunpowder filled Delia's nostrils. Their eyes, wide with disbelief and pain, met hers.

Delia, a porcelain doll with a heart of ice, leveled her weapon. The cold steel mirrored the glacial glint in her eyes.

"Tell me where Thorne is," she said, her voice a silken whisper that carried the threat of a storm. "One of you lives. Choose wisely."

Silence, thick and suffocating, hung between them. The ticking of a hidden clock became a deafening drumbeat. Delia's decision was swift, brutal. A single, precise shot silenced the man's pleas, the crimson bloom staining the polished floor. The woman's eyes, pools of desperate fear, locked onto Delia's. Delia felt a flicker of something . . . hesitation? Pity? No. Delia crushed that sentiment.

"Thorne," Delia repeated, her voice a low, dangerous hum.

The woman's hand, trembling, snaked towards the pistol at her hip. Delia's heel pressed down, bone-jarring pressure on the woman's already ravaged thigh. She choked down a scream, a raw animal sound, with her hand as tears streamed down her face, mixing with the sweat and the spreading stain of blood. Delia released the pressure, the silence amplified by the woman's ragged breaths.

"Where is Thorne?" Delia repeated, her voice devoid of warmth, each syllable a hammer blow.

"Fuck you, bitch!" the woman rasped, her defiance born of despair, of something broken and feral.

Delia felt not an ounce of remorse. Another shot, swift and merciless, ended the conversation. The stillness returned, deeper, more profound, heavy with the weight of blood and death. Thorne's location, however, remained shrouded in a silence far more menacing than any scream.

The blood slicked beneath her shoes, a grim, viscous lubricant as Delia ascended the stairs. She knew the safe room existed—a gilded cage for his darkest secrets. But where? This monstrous house, a labyrinth of shadowed hallways and echoing chambers, held its secrets close.

The bodies, a gruesome testament to the security detail's futile bravery, lay scattered like discarded toys. Their glassy eyes, frozen in the last moments of terror, burned themselves into her memory.

"He'd be here," she thought, a cold certainty gripping her.

Her heart, a frantic drumbeat against her ribs, mirrored the staccato rhythm of her steps. The cold steel of the pistol was a familiar weight in her hand, offering scant comfort against the creeping dread.

The door to the master bedroom, a monstrous slab of oak, loomed before her. She pushed it inward, the groan of protesting hinges a mournful dirge. The room, a cavern of silk and shadow, reeked of expensive cologne, a sweet counterpoint to the metallic tang of blood and the smell of gunpowder. More dead bodies were scattered about. Her breath hitched. The air itself seemed thick with the unspoken menace, with the wisps of screams. Each shadow writhed, a potential threat.

Her senses screamed, every nerve ending on high alert. She swept the room, the muzzle of her pistol a steady, unwavering finger of judgment. The stench of decay, a macabre perfume clinging to the air, warred with the sharp, cloying sweetness of Thorne's cologne. Then, a third scent, a viper slithering through the miasma—jasmine. It slammed into her, a visceral memory, a brand seared into her soul. The delicate bloom, once cherished, now twisted into a symbol of bitter betrayal, of a love poisoned and turned to ash.

As she approached the bed, the scent of jasmine intensified, a suffocating wave washing over her. The reek of death receded, drowned in the floral tide. Reason, the fragile dam she'd built against the torrent of her respect for Thorne, shattered. He was in trouble, a puppet in a meticulously orchestrated world of deceit, manipulated by a master puppeteer whose silken strings were almost invisible. This entire charade, the staged horror around her, screamed of a trap. The chilling certainty iced her veins.

Thorne's predicament was a brutal slap in the face, a revelation etched in the agonizing sweetness of jasmine. She had been blind, a pawn in someone else's treacherous game, betrayed not only by him, but by a cunning, invisible hand that had manipulated her every move. She would save him. She had to. But she knew she had been betrayed, and she would need to settle a score years in the making.

| 23 |

The Game of Shadows

Delia sat in her SUV, the leather cold against her skin, mirroring the icy dread gripping her heart. The tapestry of her life wasn't just woven with deceit; it was unraveling, thread by agonizing thread, revealing a horrifying truth she wanted to ignore. Was it the Organization, that faceless entity that had shaped her into a weapon, that had betrayed her? Or was it Elena that haunted her waking moments and tormented her sleep? The thought of Elena being alive clawed at her, a physical pain sharper than any knife.

She'd seen Elena die, saw the life drain from her, felt the sickening finality as Elena's lifeless body slipped beneath the water, knowing that it was her bullets that had ended the life of someone she loved more than life itself. The memory, vivid and visceral, was a constant, brutal reminder of her own complicity.

The problem wasn't just the possibility of Elena's survival; it was the shattering of everything Delia believed in. Their shared past, forged in the crucible of the training program, was the foundation of her identity.

Two street rats, scraping by, elevated to a position of power and influence—a power built on their symbiotic relationship. Their bond, a twisted, inextricable thing that had blossomed into something beautiful and forbidden, had been her rock, her solace, her strength. They had spent hours exploring each other's bodies, bodies that had developed into incredible specimens of womanhood.

Now that foundation crumbled beneath the weight of suspicion and betrayal. The Elena she knew, the Elena she loved, the Elena she killed, was a mask concealing a ruthless ambition. The Organization demanded absolute loyalty, unquestioning obedience. But a part of Delia, a fragile ember of her former self, screamed against the cold, logic of their mission. She'd sacrificed everything for them, committed acts she couldn't even begin to confess, that violated the core of her humanity. Yet, a chilling possibility dawned: Had she been a pawn all along, manipulated by the Organization and Elena?

The thought was unbearable. Her inner conflict raged. To uncover the truth meant facing the possibility that her entire life had been a lie, a performance designed to pit her against Elena. It meant confronting the horrifying possibility that Elena's betrayal was not a mere act of personal ambition but a intentional move within a larger game that she was already losing. It meant choosing between the loyalty she owed the Organization and her desperate hope of reclaiming the truth, even if that truth was more devastating than the betrayal itself. And the terrible, sickening truth was that she was already beginning to make choices she knew were wrong, that went against everything she once held dear, in a desperate attempt to unravel the tangled threads of her past, even if it cost her everything.

Delia's mind raced as she grappled with the agonizing realization that her life might be built on a foundation of lies. The thought of being manipulated by both the Organization and Elena was a bitter pill to swallow. She had always prided herself on her strength and loyalty, but now she questioned if those very traits had been used against her. Every memory, every shared experience with Elena, was now suspect.

The bond they had forged in the training program, the unspoken understanding between two kindred spirits rising from the streets, could have been an elaborate charade.

As Delia sat in her SUV, she knew she had to act. Unraveling this conspiracy would be her chance at redemption, no matter how painful the truth might be. She started the car, the rumble of the SUV's powerful engine echoing her determination. Her destination: the heart of the Organization, where she would demand answers.

As she drove, memories flashed before her eyes—the harsh streets of their childhood, the grueling training that forged their bond, and the missions that tested the limits of their loyalty. Every step of the way, Elena had been by her side, a source of strength and comfort. Was it all an act? The thought of Elena's potential betrayal cut deep, but it was the prospect of her own naiveté that stung the most.

Delia's hands gripped the steering wheel as she navigated the familiar route to the Organization's heart. The journey mirrored the path her thoughts were taking— a descent into the depths of her own personal hell. With each mile, her uncertainty grew heavier, and the bitter flavor of betrayal coated her mouth.

She knew that once she arrived, there would be no turning back. The answers she sought could either redeem her or destroy her. The prospect of facing the truth, of exposing the potential lies and manipulation, was terrifying. Yet, it was the idea of her own complicity, of being a pawn in a situation she couldn't control, that haunted her.

As she drew closer to her destination, the memories became more intense. She recalled the late-night conversations they'd had, the secrets they'd shared, and the dreams they'd woven together. Had it all been an act? Was Elena's love, their shared history, a mere illusion designed to control her? The thought of her own naiveté, of being manipulated, filled her with a rage that burned away the last vestiges of hesitation. She would get her answers, and if the truth proved to be as ugly as she feared, she would unleash that rage upon those who had used her.

| 24 |

The Cost of Loyalty

The cool night air, thick with the scent of salt and brine, kissed Elena's skin as she slipped from the bed. Thorne's breath, a slow, rhythmic rasp, was the only sound in the sea-themed bedroom, a counterpoint to the frantic drumbeat of her heart.

His exhaustion, a delicious vulnerability, was her weapon. She savored it, the way his body, still warm from their brutal coupling, molded itself to the silk sheets, a landscape she knew intimately, a landscape she would soon betray.

She slid from under the sheets and stepped to the French doors that led to the deck. She pushed them open, revealing a panorama of glittering ocean, a billion diamonds scattered across velvet black. The moonlight, cold and sharp, etched shadows across her naked body, highlighting the tremor in her hand as she gripped the balcony railing.

The past two days had been a blur of adrenaline and acceptable risk. A ballet of death played out against the backdrop of their daring escape. The penthouse, the mansion, swallowed by the Organization's relentless assault—all orchestrated, all falling into her bloody design. Two guards remained. Mere inconveniences. Thorne, with his access codes, was the prize, a prize she would claim before silencing him.

Delia's unexpected arrival had both thrilled and chilled her. Years of silent, parallel operations, their paths crossing like venomous snakes in the shadows, memories of longing and betrayal, now an inconvenient variable in her equation. The residual warmth of their shared history burned against the ice of her ambition. Yes, she still felt it, a flicker of something akin to love, a poisoned ember that fueled the cold calculation in her eyes. It wouldn't stop her. Delia would be her ultimate sacrifice, a lover's quarrel between Delia and Thorne escalating to a symphony of screams and death.

A wave of heat flooded her, a visceral memory of Delia's touch, of forbidden fruit in their youth. She traced the curves of her breasts in her mind, the hardened tips of her nipples a testament to the simmering hunger within. The need, sharp and primal, pulled her back into the room, a silent predator returning to its prey.

She slid beneath the sheets, her fingers finding their way between Thorne's legs, his response instant and eager. His surrender was bittersweet. As sleep claimed her, a single thought snaked its way through her mind, a venomous whisper: Delia. She owed her everything, and yet, she would kill her. It was the price of victory, the cost of a dream. Her thoughts turned to that final mission.

The stale air had hung thick with the metallic tang of blood, a scent that clung to Delia like a second skin. It was the first time they'd hunted together; the Organization, its icy grip tightening with each whispered command, had deemed this mission too crucial for divided forces.

Their quarry: a butcher from a bygone hell, a concentration camp commandant who'd fled the crumbling Reich, finding sanctuary—and obscene wealth—in the unsuspecting heart of Baltimore. He'd built a gilded cage for himself and his oblivious family, but the beast within remained unsated. He'd woven himself into the fabric of power, a spider spinning a net of treachery, his influence a venomous tendril reaching into the highest echelons of American politics.

The Organization's decree: extermination. A job for a squad, not a single assassin. But Delia and Elena, two shadows moving as one, had slithered into his opulent world. Their seduction was a symphony of whispers and charm, a slow, agonizing dance towards the inevitable.

They had systematically dismantled his inner circle, each kill a chilling echo in the opulent silence of his mansion. Then, something shifted within Elena. Her gaze, laser-focused on their shared target, snagged on something else—a relic, a treasure salvaged from the ashes of the Fatherland: a religious scroll, a thing of incandescent beauty and unimaginable value. It was a siren song, its hypnotic allure eclipsing their mission, twisting Elena's soul. She would abandon everything—the Organization, their shared purpose, even Delia—for this object, this promise of a new life far removed from blood and betrayal.

***

Delia felt the icy dread slithering into her own veins, the taste of betrayal metallic on her tongue. Her last encounter with Elena was a traumatic. Elena's betrayal was swift, merciless, delivered with the cold precision of a surgeon. Delia had been left for dead, the warm sticky slick of her wounds a brutal counterpoint to the chilling click of the guards' approaching boots.

Elena, having plundered the sacred scroll from the safe, left Delia at the mercy of the snarling men. The screams of their dying still echoed in her ears, a chorus of agony. Delia, fueled by a potent cocktail of rage and adrenaline, had escaped.

The city blurred around her, a maelstrom of swirling lights and shadows. The chase was fueled by revenge, her ragged breathing was a harsh counterpoint to the relentless pounding of her heart.

She'd found Elena on a rain-slicked bridge, its skeletal frame looming over the churning blackness of the river below. Their final confrontation was a brutal, silent explosion of violence. The shots rang out, sharp cracks in the stillness of the night, followed by a gasp, blood oozing from multiple locations on Elena's white blouse and a sickening thud as Elena plunged into the inky depths. Delia stared as her lover, her friend, her partner in darkness, vanished into the abyss. The river swallowed her whole. The cold, indifferent water reflected the cold, indifferent sky, leaving Delia standing alone, the weight of the world crushing her chest. It wasn't just Elena's life that had ended on that bridge; a part of Delia died there too sinking with her into the cold, unforgiving embrace of the river.

The icy wind of that night still clawed at Delia even after all these years, a cold touch mirroring the chill that had settled in her bones the night Elena died. Elena, whose body the black, churning water had stolen, and who never returned, left the echoing splash in her ears and the smell of blood on Delia's hands—a scent that clung, a grim perfume of her guilt. Each shot, precise and deadly, played out again in her mind. The only thing remaining was the scent of jasmine in the air.

"My shots were true," she whispered.

Elena's death, a gaping wound in her soul, had silenced the reckless passion that had once burned between them, a passion now replaced by a cold, unwavering grief. She'd never forgiven herself and never forgotten. The Organization had saved her that night, but there was always the question of what happened on that bridge that night. All they had was Delia's account of the events leading to that fateful night and the fact that Delia had taken the life of one of their very best assets.

The betrayal was bitter, a vile concoction brewing in her gut. Had the Organization manipulated her feelings for Thorne, that smoldering ember of connection, that warmth against the arctic chill of her loss? Was Thorne a tool, a pawn in their insidious bout? Or had Elena, from beyond the grave, somehow orchestrated this cruel betrayal? The thought sent a jolt of icy dread through her: Elena, ever the enigmatic manipulator, even in death. A death now in question.

Delia had dedicated her life to purging the world of the "scumbags" who twisted reality to their perverse designs, yet she was drowning in a sea of her own making. And whoever had betrayed her, whoever had played her like a violin, would face the full, merciless fury of Delia's wrath. Let them pray for mercy; they wouldn't find any.

| 25 |

A Dangerous Revelation

The dawn bled gold onto the silk sheets, a grotesque parody of the sunrise Elena cherished. The air was thick with the scent of expensive linens and something else . . . something foreboding, that hung heavy in the simple bedroom.

Naked, she stood a goddess of vengeance in the doorway, the ocean's turquoise expanse a cruel mockery of the serene beauty she'd once found in it. Even the shapeless sweatshirt couldn't hide the curves that whispered of a power both alluring and deadly. Her fingers, tracing the bone-handled knife she pulled from beneath the mattress, felt the faintest tremor of anticipation. The blood bloomed on her tongue as she licked the tiny wound—a prelude to the main course.

Thorne, oblivious, snored softly. The rhythmic rise and fall of his chest was a maddening metronome, counting down to her liberation.

"So easy," she said, the knife glinting, a sliver of moonlight in the dim room. "One swift stroke, and I'm free. Home. Rich beyond measure."

She slid the knife up the sleeve of her sweatshirt, its cold kiss against her skin a promise kept. She left the bedroom and walked into the kitchen. Jefferson, one of the two remaining security guards who had helped them escape the mansions during the blitz attack, stood at the coffee maker. He was a hulking brute with eyes that held a flicker of fear beneath their practiced nonchalance, waiting for his cup to finish filling.

Elena entered, her presence a storm brewing in the otherwise tranquil kitchen. The coffee's rich aroma warred with the jasmine clinging to her. She saw his gaze linger. The baggy fabric strained against her ample breasts, a taunt. Jasmine, a deceptive perfume, masked the scent of her intent. She took the pot, her fingers brushing his. A silent challenge.

"Peters?" she asked.

"Asleep. Night shift. You're stuck with me." His voice, a gravelly rasp, betrayed his discomfort.

Elena filled her cup, walked to the kitchen door, opened it and stepped onto the stone patio. Outside, the ocean was a vast, indifferent abyss. She stepped off the patio and walked to the edge of the cliff.

"Jefferson," she called, her voice a silken whisper laced with ice, "can you come here for a second?"

He walked to where she was standing. He took a sip of coffee, the dark liquid mirroring the shadow in her eyes. "Yes, ma'am?"

The attack was a blur of motion, as the knife, a silver serpent, found its mark in his thigh with sickening ease. The crashing waves swallowed his cry as she spun, driving the blade deep into the base of his skull. Without hesitation, she pulled him to the precipice, his lifeblood staining her hands. A crimson baptism. She pushed him off the edge.

She watched his body plummet, the ocean a final, unforgiving embrace. The knife, cleaned on the coarse cliff grass, was almost pristine. She slid it back up her sleeve. She picked up his abandoned coffee cup, its warmth a stark contrast to the cold purpose that filled her. The taste of victory? Perhaps.

The sun had risen higher now, casting an unforgiving light on the scene of her latest handiwork. Elena, a vision of deadly grace, stood at the precipice, the wind whipping her hair into a wild tangle. The coppery flavor still lingered on her tongue, a bitter reminder of the violence she had wrought. But there was no remorse, just a cold satisfaction as she stared down at the rocks below. The ocean, once a source of peace, now mirrored the darkness in her soul, its relentless tide washing away the evidence of her deed.

She turned, her eyes narrowing at the sight of Thorne, who was still unaware of the danger that had lurked so close. A muscle twitched in her jaw, indicating a storm raging within. Thorne, a mere pawn in her game of survival, would be her next target. But first, she needed to ensure her escape, to craft the deception and leave no trace of her true intentions.

The beach house, with its sun-drenched bedrooms and tranquil patios, now felt like a prison from which she had to escape. Every second spent within its walls was a threat, a reminder that her freedom was still precarious. As she made her way back inside, her steps purposeful, she knew that her true liberation was yet to come. Thorne was her ticket out, and only then would she feel like she was home. Elena walked back to the house and entered the kitchen. Thorne was seated at the table, sipping his coffee.

"Where is everyone?" he asked.

Elena smiled. "I think Peters covered the night shift, so he must be sleeping. Not sure where Jefferson is, maybe patrolling the grounds."

She sat opposite him. "We need to come up with a plan, sweetheart. As nice as this place is, eventually someone is going to figure out your connection to it and we will face another assault."

"What do you suggest?" he asked.

"The first thing we need to do is get the access codes for Nexus so we can make sure they're secure. Then we need to get on your jet and get out of this country. I know several places we can go where you will be safe and able to live your life in luxury."

Thorne studied her for a few seconds. "Why are you so focused on me getting the codes? The codes are safe, and once I release Nexus to the public, I will set it up so that the codes are unnecessary."

"You're not looking at the big picture. The money you make from selling Nexus will give you everything you ever wanted, and you can spend your money on anything you want, including making the world a better place."

Thorne laughed. "I don't need more money. Nexus will level the world's playing fields and every country will have access to the information on it. We will all be safer because of me. Détente."

Elena stood up, walked to the coffee maker, poured herself another cup and turned to face him.

"For a guy who is so smart, you're naïve as hell. Look around you, Thorne. People are trying to kill you for what you have, or they're trying to kill you for what you intend to do. Either way, you will be just as dead. Grow the fuck up and get rid of this idealistic dream. Your app is worth billions. We need to sell it as soon as possible, like today, and get the fuck out of here. Once you sell it, no one will bother you. We need those codes."

Thorne had never seen her like this, and he wasn't sure what to think. He wasn't sure if she was still on his side or not. A thought crossed his mind. "I can kill the app right now, and it won't be worth anything to anyone." He would need to mull that around in his mind. He also needed to keep a closer eye on Elena.

| 26 |

The Edge of Betrayal

The driveway of the nondescript house three blocks from the Santa Monica shore swallowed retired Supreme Court Justice Harold Walker's car. He switched off the ignition, the silence amplifying the emptiness within him. Again, the house remained shrouded in darkness, a symbolic reflection of his internal state since Meredith's passing five years prior. Lung cancer had stolen his wife, his life's companion of four decades, leaving behind the scent of vanilla—a culinary memory haunting the empty rooms, a cruel reminder of her warmth and the delectable surprises she'd once baked. The house, once vibrant with her presence, now echoed with the desolate clang of his solitude.

He retrieved the newspaper from the stoop, the rustling pages a fragile counterpoint to the crushing weight of his weariness. The weariness etched onto his face mirrored the burdens he carried. He settled his briefcase onto the entry table, a silent testament to a career that now felt hollow. The refrigerator offered meager inspiration for dinner; his appetite, like his spirit, had waned. A drink, he decided, was the only palatable option. The living room's lights revealed a familiar scene, yet one that was about to be irrevocably shattered. He reached for the decanter, the amber liquid promising a momentary escape.

"Perhaps a double would be more suitable," a voice cut through the stillness.

Harold whirled around, the glass slipping from his grasp, shattering on the polished floor. A chilling smile played on Delia's lips as she sat poised in a high-backed chair near the fireplace, a silenced pistol resting in her lap, aimed squarely at him.

"What the fuck are you doing here?" His voice was a strangled whisper.

"A conversation, I believe, is overdue," Delia replied, her tone laced with lethal calm. "Considering your three previous attempts to kill me."

She gestured with the weapon towards a high-backed chair in the corner, her eyes unwavering.

"Please have a seat." He obeyed, his gaze riveted on the cold steel.

"How did you find me?"

"That's what you trained me to do, Justice Walker. Find people and kill them. Tell me. How long have you known she was still alive?"

"Who is alive?" he asked.

Without a flicker of movement, Delia squeezed the trigger. The bullet ripped through the air, embedding itself mere inches from his head in the chair's back Terror seized him.

"Focus, Director," Delia commanded, her voice steely. "How long have you known Elena was alive?"

Justice Walker, the director of the Organization, looked at her steely gaze. "I thought she was dead. She died on that bridge in Baltimore. You saw it yourself."

"Obviously, something changed," said Delia, "since she is now in the company of the man you sent me to kill. What changed?"

Delia shifted the barrel of the pistol a little to the left, and the director's eyes grew wide.

"I don't know what changed, Delia, I swear. I believed she was dead until she appeared here, much as you have, a couple of months back, sitting in that same chair, pistol extended. That was the first time I had seen her since before that night on the bridge."

"What is her game?" she asked.

The director hesitated, and Delia raised the tip of the barrel. He pushed deeper into the chair.

"She offered me a proposition. She represents a group that is interested in the Nexus app. They were willing to pay me a huge bonus if I could get the app for them. Part of the deal, though, was that you had to die."

"Who is this group she represents?"

"I have no idea," said the director. "I imagine they are a foreign interest. She never said. All she said was money was no object."

"You sent people to kill Thorne. How was she planning to get the access codes to the app if he was dead?"

The director looked around the room like he was looking for an escape. Delia pulled the trigger, and a second bullet hit the wing of the chair, this one closer than the first. He leaned to one side. His eyes were wide with fear. Delia shifted the barrel to the left.

"The next one goes in your head," she said. Her voice was as cold as steel and showed no emotion.

"All right, all right. Don't think for a second we wanted Thorne dead. Her clients wanted Nexus, but they also want Thorne."

The stench of his betrayal hung heavy in the air, thick as the smoke from a burning pyre. "Our plan was a slow squeeze. Make him believe his life was a flickering candle, about to be snuffed out. Force him into the light. Elena was supposed to be your executioner. You were just a cog in the plan. She was to silence you before you could reach him, before you could . . . help him. But then you saw him, didn't you? That glint in his eyes, that desire to save the world . . . a fascination took hold, a poisonous bloom in the garden of your obsession. And he became infatuated with you. A mistake in our plan. Thorne, the arrogant fool, wouldn't give up the codes, not even to Elena, despite their . . . intimacy. So, she used you. To leverage your . . . infatuation. He never knew you were supposed to kill him. She had convinced him you were there to steal the files, but she was running out of time, her clients growing impatient. I arranged for the attack on the penthouse and on the mansion to push him over the edge. At that point, Elena revealed your true intentions, so he was more willing to flee with her."

Disbelief choked Delia. The fury clawing at her chest wasn't a simmer; it was a wildfire consuming everything.

"People died, you monster! Innocent people! Your own people! Loyal to the bone, and you tossed them aside like trash. Betrayed them all . . . and me. For what?"

His smile, accompanied by a predatory gleam in his eyes, was a physical affront. The reek of his arrogance filled the air, thick and suffocating.

"Money, Delia. More than you can fathom. The means to create a new life, far from my pursuers. Come with me. Now that you know the plan, you can eliminate Elena, and we can vanish. Her clients will take care of your . . . needs."

The shot, silent and deadly, ended the conversation. The scent of cordite stung her nostrils as his skull exploded, the sickening crunch a final insult to her ears. His body slumped, a grotesque parody of the power he'd wielded. Delia felt the hot steel of the pistol, a searing brand against her palm.

The betrayal sliced deeper than any bullet. Years. A lifetime of blind faith in a man who'd seen her as nothing more than a pawn, a disposable piece in his depraved game. The tremor in her hand wasn't just from the adrenaline; it was the weight of shattered ideals, the cold, crushing realization that the father figure she'd worshipped was a fraud. Tears, hot and stinging, blurred her vision.

She wiped them away with the back of her hand. She holstered the weapon, its cold steel a stark contrast to the burning rage that consumed her. She had to find Elena and Thorne. She had to stop them before it was too late. The search of the house was futile. She found nothing that would lead her to the pair. Despair, sharp and cold as a winter wind, pierced through her. She walked into the kitchen and turned on every gas burner. She found a small metal pan, placed it in the microwave and set the timer— ten minutes to obliterate every trace of Harold Walker, his legacy and her own complicity in his bloody reign. Then she vanished, leaving the scent of gas and the chilling whisper of vengeance in her wake.

| 27 |

A New Plan

Seeking refuge in her secluded apartment, a sanctuary from recent events, Delia slumped onto the well-worn leather sofa. A half-empty bottle of beer sat forgotten beside her, its contents almost an afterthought to the mesmerizing flicker of the fireplace. The flames' hypnotic sway mirrored the tempest raging inside her.

Uncharacteristic of her refined palate, the beer's mild bitterness proved insufficient solace, but the potent sting of bourbon chased with the lager was a necessary antidote to her numb despair. The liquid's searing passage down her throat, a visceral counterpoint to her emotional paralysis, offered a fragile, bitter relief.

Her mission was a viper coiled around her soul, its fangs dripping with the venom of conflicting desires, a bitter contrast to the touch of Thorne's lips—a forbidden sweetness that burned like acid. She'd known from the outset that her feelings were a catastrophic flaw, a crack in the icy façade she'd meticulously crafted. But his presence, a magnetic storm of charisma and hidden vulnerability, had shattered her defenses, drawing her into a maelstrom of achieving his goals.

The director, a creature of chilling pragmatism and merciless ambition, had been her architect since her brutal training. His voice, a rasp of ice and steel, echoed in the darkest chambers of her mind. His words were a poisoned chalice, a gilded cage offering a freedom she could never attain. The betrayal felt like a physical violation, a rape of her spirit.

"Money, Delia. More than you can fathom. The means to create a new life, far from my pursuers. Come with me.

Now that you know the plan, you can eliminate Elena, and we can vanish. Her clients will take care of your . . . needs."

She was no mere automaton, no pawn on some grand chessboard. The agony of his betrayal clawed at her throat, constricting her breath, choking the life from her. The very notion was a rebellion burning in her veins, a wildfire consuming her.

She'd risked everything for the Organization—her freedom, her identity, her very soul—and found out that money and power could replace that loyalty.

Delia stared at the flames, their movement becoming a reflection of her internal struggle. She had answers, but she needed clarity. The director's motives, the secrets he'd held, were veiled in shadows. Her own past, the events that had shaped her into the ruthless assassin she'd become, whispered haunting truths in the back of her mind.

The tension in the safe house intensified. Delia knew she couldn't stay hidden. She needed to confront the situation head-on. She needed to find answers, to unravel the deceit that threatened to consume her.

As she rose, a steely glint in her eyes, she knew the path ahead would be treacherous. She would face danger and try not to lose everything she held dear. But she was Delia Cahill, a woman who lived on the edge, a woman who played in the shadows with her life on the line. And she would not back down.

Delia opened the cabinet and pulled out a black duffel bag. She picked through her weapons and filled the bag with those items she felt would be needed to complete the mission. A mission not to kill Thorne, but to save him from Elena.

She stripped off her clothes and slid into the black pants and shirt that would protect her in the night. She laced up her boots, slipped her knives into the attached sheaths and slid her pistol into the holster under her arm. She finished her beer and left the apartment, possibly for the last time. She had a thought where she might find Elena and Thorne, but she needed to go to his penthouse to find the answer.

| 28 |

A Moment of Clarity

Delia stood across the street from the building that housed Thorne's penthouse, protected from the rain by a canvas awning, watching the building as the storm drenched the area. She had hoped that Thorne and Elena might have returned to the penthouse, but she understood now that the penthouse was no longer a safe space for Thorne and that they would never be returning. And that was okay. What she needed was inside, and she hoped it would give her the answers that she needed to find Thorne and Elena. Her reflection stared back at her from the mist-covered window, the harsh streetlight illuminating the stark lines of her face. The woman who looked back was a stranger, a spectre of the life she used to have. Her life before the shadows, before the training, before the kill.

She hadn't always been this woman, the woman who could disappear into the night, vanish without a trace, leaving but a whisper of her presence. She used to be just Delia, a nameless face in a sea of ordinary lives.

It had been a long time since she'd allowed herself to delve into those memories, the memories of a life that existed before her metamorphosis. Her husband, David, would never understand the duality of her existence. To him, she was a picture of contentment, a woman who found joy in being part of his life. But she was also a highpowered professional who kept billionaires under her thumb as she handled their legal affairs. She played the role flawlessly, or at least he thought she did. She'd mastered the art of deception, the ability to conceal the darkness within, to keep it at bay.

She was tired. Tired of the constant vigilance, tired of the deception, tired of the loneliness. She craved normalcy, a life without shadows, without the constant threat of death. But her reality was one of endless nights, the world outside her window a blurry mosaic of neon signs and speeding cars.

The rain lashed against the window, blurring her reflection into a grotesque parody—a fun-house mirror showcasing the fractured soul within. The chill seeped through the glass, mirroring the icy dread that clenched her heart. A cacophony of screams—the screams of her conscience—echoed in her skull, a brutal orchestration of duty and desire, betrayal and loyalty. She had to bridge the chasm, to forge a path where her life and her oath didn't annihilate each other, even if it meant shattering the very foundations of her existence. This knife-edge walk demanded everything.

Pulling her hood tight, a damp chill clinging to the fabric, she sprinted across the rain-slicked street, each footfall a thunderclap in the tempest. The stale air of the lobby hit her like a physical blow. The young guard, a coiled spring of muscle and alertness, looked up—

recognition, a flicker of something akin to . . . fear darting across his face. His hand snaked towards the drawer, but he was too slow.

The silenced shot was a whisper, a brutal punctuation to his life. A second clinical shot to the head silenced any lingering possibility. She stripped the weapon from his lifeless grip, the cold steel heavy in her hand, discarding the magazine and the chambered shell in the trash with a practiced indifference. Was he from the Organization or was he working for Elena? It didn't matter. It was all a venomous tangle of snakes now; the distinctions were meaningless.

With the director's death, she had rewritten the rules. This was a new game, and she was playing it by her own rules. The pistol remained in her hand, a cold, reassuring weight, as she stepped into the elevator, its metallic sheen reflecting her determined, ruthless gaze. The penthouse loomed. The game had begun.

| 29 |

Deceitful Allies

The penthouse elevator hissed open, a metallic groan that sliced through the suffocating silence. Two figures, hulking silhouettes against the stark light, stood braced. Their feet, planted wide, were rooted to the polished floor; the cold steel of their weapons pressed heavy against their palms, a metallic chill that mirrored the icy dread in their eyes. They were statues, sculpted from tension, trained killing machines . . . until the silence stretched, a taut rubber band threatening to snap.

"What the fuck?" asked one guard.

The words, a guttural rasp, ripped through the air. His partner nodded, a flicker of unease in his eyes—a crack in his unwavering professionalism. Before he could react, the doors started to close, a mechanical hiss that was a prelude to violence.

Delia, a blur of motion, launched herself through the closing gap, sliding across the polished floor on her belly. Four dull cracks followed, hitting both guards in their knees. The guards' legs buckled, their bodies collapsing like marionettes whose strings had been severed. The air throbbed with the staccato bursts of their pistols, shots fired wildly into the walls and ceiling as they fell.

Delia stood, a grim reaper in tailored black, her breath ragged. She put a bullet into each guard's head and then she stopped. Silence descended again, heavy and expectant. She listened, her senses straining—the silence was a liar, a deceptive calm before the storm. It held no promise of rescue. Her gun remained raised, a leaden extension of her arm, as she moved through the penthouse, clearing each room with practiced efficiency.

The master bedroom was a testament to a savage battle. The remnants of a once-impenetrable door lay scattered, splintered wood and twisted metal forming a macabre landscape. Her gaze fell on a ripped-away panel, revealing a hidden staircase leading to the roof and the safety of a waiting helicopter—a desperate escape route, meticulously concealed. A bitter laugh escaped her lips.

"So that's how they were able to escape."

She left the bedroom and crossed the apartment, moving towards the art vault with its sealed door, her heart a lead weight in her chest. The painting she sought hopefully held the key to her revenge. The vault door gaped open, its security system a mangled mess of wires and torn metal. Relief, sharp and sudden, pierced the grim determination that had held her together.

The paintings, priceless masterpieces, remained untouched. She stepped over the mangled door and turned on the lights. She walked around the room until she came to the picture she was looking for. Thorne had specifically shown her this picture during her visit. A beautiful painting of a distinctive beach house somewhere along the California coastline, a storm brewing in the background.

"Could it be this easy?" she asked herself. "Of all his masterpieces, he showed me this painting by an unknown artist. Does it hold some significance?"

She leaned closer and looked at the signature on the bottom. Doris Thorne. Delia smiled. The picture was painted by his mother or grandmother. The house was most likely a family property, and perhaps the perfect place to hide.

She pulled out her phone and opened the Google images app. She took a picture of the painting and posted it. Within seconds, her phone chimed. The image on her screen was an exact duplicate of the house in the painting. The app gave her the address of the house, and she plugged it into her Google Maps program. The directions filled her screen, and she knew she needed to get a move on if she was going to make it by morning. Delia slipped her phone back into her pocket and stepped out of the vault. She had a destination. Now all she had to hope was that Thorne and Elena were there, or this would be a waste of time.

Delia stepped past the two lifeless bodies on the floor and pushed the elevator button. The doors slid open, and she stepped into the cab. As the elevators opened on the ground floor, she stepped back and waited a few seconds to make sure there was no waiting party. Confident, she stepped out, holstered her pistol and walked out the front doors, disappearing into the night.

| 30 |

The Plot Thickens

The air in the sterile office was thick with tension, a palpable energy that hummed beneath the surface of the sleek, modern furniture. The man on the opposite side of the desk, Secretary of Defense Carl Reynolds, activated the SCIF, the sensitive compartmented information facility, and he felt a noticeable change in the atmosphere in the room. He felt his ears pop as the security measures engaged, sealing the room tight from electronic eavesdropping. He had been a part of meetings like this in the past, but never on his own. He was always part of a team. The SECDEF read through the report, his steely gaze unwavering as he looked at the latest intel. The conspiracy, it revealed, was far more intricate than they had believed.

"This isn't just about eliminating a rogue tech billionaire," the SECDEF said, his voice a low growl. "It's about controlling the world."

His mind raced, trying to grasp the enormity of what the SECDEF said. He knew Delia had been conditioned to focus on individual targets, executing them with clinical precision, but this—this was a whole new level of danger.

"The network is vast," the SECDEF continued, his words a cold, measured drip of truth. "It reaches into governments, corporations, even the military. They are a silent force, pulling strings from the shadows, and our target—he was just the tip of the iceberg."

The information the SECDEF revealed was explosive. The billionaire's app wasn't just a revolutionary tool for tracking submarines, it was the key to controlling global communication networks, a weapon capable of manipulating information, disseminating propaganda and fracturing the world into a chaotic, fractured landscape. No nation on earth would be safe once the app was released, which was why the Organization, and in particular, Delia, had been assigned to stop that from happening. But something changed. He felt a wave of nausea wash over him. The magnitude of what she had stumbled upon was terrifying.

Thorne was not just a target. He was a shield, a safeguard against a force far more sinister than she could have imagined. The SECDEF's words resonated in the silence that followed.

"This is not just about her assignment anymore, it's about preventing a global catastrophe."

The weight of responsibility pressed down on him, a crushing weight he had never known before. His world, like hers, was divided between the mundane and the deadly but had become a tangled mess of conflicting emotions and impossible choices.

Thorne was not a pawn. He was a player, a cunning strategist who had been playing his own game for years, his every move designed to achieve a specific goal. And Delia had no idea that she was now a part of this game.

The more they learned about him, the more they questioned their initial assessment. Was he the enemy? Was he the one pulling the strings, orchestrating this global game of power? Or was he, as he appeared, a victim of circumstance, a man who had been manipulated by a force far larger than himself?

The lines between right and wrong had become blurred beyond recognition. She would find herself in a moral quagmire, her very soul a battlefield for conflicting ideologies.

"The death of the director has really fucked this up," said the SECDEF. "Do we have any idea what he was doing?"

The man looked across the desk. "As best we can determine, he was running a side op. We know he met with a woman at his club. We don't know who she is or what part she plays in all this. We also know that Delia was seen leaving his house just prior to the explosion and fire. We know the director was shot in the head before the explosion. I had asked him once to give Delia the benefit of the doubt, but now I don't know what to think. We don't know if she was part of what was going on or if she was still just a pawn. She killed him for a reason."

The SECDEF looked across the desk. He held up the picture of the woman from the director's club. "Use whatever resources you need, but find out who this woman is and what her involvement is. We have no idea when Thorne intends to release the app, but we need to do whatever we can to prevent that from happening."

He hesitated for a moment, his eyes narrowing. "Use all the assets of the Organization and find Delia. She needs to be eliminated. And find out what the director was involved in."

The SECDEF placed all the documents from his desk into a shredder and pushed the button. The grinding noise filled the room. He pushed the button on the desk console, opening the sealed shades and unsealing the door. The meeting was over, but a lot of work remained. The man stood and left the office.

| 31 |

The Choice

Back in the safety of her apartment, Delia sat at the kitchen table listening to the rhythmic drumming of rain against the windows, the dim light of the single lamp casting long, menacing shadows across the floor. The remnants of a dinner that had gone uneaten lay scattered before her, a stark reminder of the sudden shift in her world.

A wave of nausea washed over her, and she pressed her hand to her stomach, trying to quell the churning within. The events of the past few hours had taken their toll, their aftermath seeping into her bones, leaving her feeling pissed. An icy dread that gnawed at the edges of her resolve had replaced the exhilaration of defying her superiors, of taking a gamble that could cost her everything.

She had betrayed them. The Organization that had been her family, her sanctuary in a world she barely recognized. And for what? For a man she had just met, a man whose enigmatic nature and hidden secrets drew her in like a moth to a flame. His very presence had disrupted her double life, leaving her teetering on the brink of an abyss.

A sudden crash of thunder shook the apartment, echoing the turmoil within Delia. The storm outside mirrored the tempest raging inside her, a storm of fear, guilt and an intoxicating blend of love and doubt. The consequences of her actions, once abstract threats lurking in the shadows, now loomed over her, palpable and menacing.

She hadn't expected the swiftness of the Organization's response. It was as if they had been expecting her betrayal, waiting for the moment she would falter to unleash their wrath upon her. The phone call from her mentor, a woman she trusted and respected, had been devoid of the usual warmth, replaced by a chilling tone that sent a shiver down her spine.

"Delia, you've crossed a line." Her mentor's voice, usually calm and measured, had been tight with suppressed fury. "You're treading on thin ice. Your defiance has consequences, consequences that will reverberate far beyond your own life. You understand what this means, don't you?"

Delia had fought to maintain her composure, but her voice had betrayed her. "I understood the risks," she replied, her voice trembling. "But I made my choice."

"You defied us, Delia. You put our mission, our entire operation, at risk."

The accusation hung heavy in the air. It was true. The director's quiet strength, the glimpses of vulnerability he had shown her, had chipped away at the icy walls she had erected. He was an enigma, a man who seemed to exist in two worlds, a world of technological brilliance and a world of dark secrets.

"The director betrayed me," she said, her voice tight with fear. She told her mentor what the director had told her in his final minutes of life. There was silence on the other end of the phone.

"There is no turning back, Delia. You have played your last card."

The threat hung in the air, a silent promise of retribution. And now, as she sat in the desolate quiet of her kitchen, the full weight of that promise crushed down upon her.

Delia opened the back of the phone and removed the battery and the SIM card. She threw them in the trash. No matter the circumstances, she had crossed a line, a line that had no going back. The consequences of her actions were now a reality, a reality she had to face.

She had betrayed the Organization, but she had also placed David in the crosshairs. He had lied to her, but he was her responsibility, her burden. The realization hit her like a physical blow. She had to make this right. He was too good, too innocent to understand the world she lived in, a world where good and evil blurred, where the line between right and wrong was a fragile, shifting boundary.

She took a deep breath, trying to steady herself. She knew what she needed to do, and she needed to do it before the Organization could stop her. She had one stop to make. She looked around the apartment. It had served her well, but there was nothing here of importance to her. She turned off the lights and walked out the door towards an uncertain future.

| 32 |

A Haunting Memory

Delia stood at the edge of the abandoned warehouse in silent refection, the wind whipping at her hair, a silent observer of the scene unfolding before her. The warehouse was the secret training base for the Organization, the place that had molded her into the killer she had become. The place where it all began. Where she had first met the director, the heart of the Organization.

Two figures lay sprawled on the concrete floor, their lives extinguished by the cold precision of her blade. Her heart, however, remained untouched, a callous shell hardened by years of training and countless executions. She was a weapon, a tool, a shadow; her name, her identity, were irrelevant to the world she inhabited. But tonight, a single memory flickered in her mind, breaking through the impenetrable wall of her indifference. It was a memory of a different life, one she had erased from her consciousness, buried beneath layers of pain and self-loathing. A life filled with warmth, laughter and the sweet embrace of a loving family. A life ripped away, leaving behind an empty void that only the icy embrace of death could fill.

The memory was an echo of a childhood spent in a quaint home nestled in a valley bathed in the golden light of a setting sun. It was a haven of innocence, a place where laughter floated on the wind and dreams soared on the wings of imagination. There, young Delia, with eyes as bright as the summer sky and a heart overflowing with laughter, had lived a life filled with simple joys. Her parents, their faces etched with love and devotion, had nurtured her dreams and shielded her from the harsh realities of the world.

But then the storm arrived, shattering the fragile peace of their existence. It started subtly, a chilling premonition that cast a shadow over their days. Soon, the whispers grew into shouts, the fear into terror, and the shadow into a suffocating darkness that consumed their lives.

Delia remembered the night the world as she knew it came crashing down. It was a night cloaked in the heavy stillness of a storm brewing on the horizon. Her mother's frantic shouts had woken her, her eyes wide with terror, her voice trembling with fear. Her father, his face pale and strained, stood at the door, his hands trembling as he held a crumpled letter. The words on the page, scrawled in bold, cold letters, were the harbingers of their doom.

The letter was a threat, a warning that spelled the end of their peaceful existence. It spoke of a debt owed, a debt they could not repay. It spoke of consequences, of a fate worse than death for those who dared to defy. Fear, thick and suffocating, filled their small home, clinging to them like the damp mist that rolled in from the valley.

The next day, the storm broke. It was a violent, destructive force that swept through their lives, leaving behind a trail of shattered dreams and broken hearts. Armed men, their faces obscured by masks, descended upon their home, shattering the windows, splintering the furniture and tearing their lives apart.

From her hiding place under the floor, Delia had witnessed her father being dragged away, his pleas for mercy falling on deaf ears. Her mother, her face contorted in death, lay broken and bloody on the kitchen floor.

Delia's world was shattered by the brutal violence. The fear, the terror, the pain—it all fused into a single burning sensation that consumed her. The world as she knew it had vanished, replaced by a cold, unforgiving reality that stripped her of her innocence and shattered her dreams.

The deaths of her mother and father left Delia alone and adrift in a sea of grief and despair. Abandoned and forgotten, she was left to navigate the treacherous currents of life, forced to navigate the shadows, to become the very monster her parents had tried to shield her from.

She was saved by the director, who found her in a juvenile facility, a young woman filled with hatred and defiance. He saw something in her she had never seen in herself. Under his tutelage, she was trained, molded, transformed into a weapon, a tool of vengeance, her spirit tempered by the fires of pain and loss. The world she had once known, the world of warmth and laughter, was replaced by a world of cold steel and silenced screams.

Delia's past, a painful scar etched deep within her soul, served as a constant reminder of everything that had been taken from her. It was a burden she carried with her, a weight that pulled her down, threatening to drown her in the depths of despair. But it was also a driving force, a burning ember of vengeance that fueled her every action, her every breath.

Tonight, standing in the shadows of the abandoned warehouse, she could feel the ghosts of her past hovering over her. They whispered tales of love, loss and betrayal. They reminded her of the path she had been forced to walk. But they also offered a glimmer of hope, a flickering candle in the darkness. A chance to find redemption, to break free from the chains that bound her to the shadows and embrace the possibility of a life reborn.

The memory faded, leaving behind a lingering chill that clung to her like a shroud. She turned away from the scene of her latest execution, her steps firm and deliberate, her gaze fixed on the horizon, determination lighting her eyes. She was a survivor, a woman forged in the fires of pain and loss, a woman determined to break free from the chains that held her captive.

Delia ripped open the black duffel. Inside lay the meticulously crafted packages, each a ticking heart of vengeance. Her fingers, calloused and scarred, traced the cold, smooth surfaces. The warehouse echoed with the low thrum of her movements, a counterpoint to the frantic hammering of her own pulse. She placed the devices, each a silent promise of retribution, in their ordained spots and synched the timers.

The duffel bag slung across her shoulder, heavy with the weight of consequence, felt less like cargo and more like a living thing pulsing with the energy of her rage. She paused at the door, the damp chill clinging to her like a shroud, a stark reminder of the thoughts that haunted her. But this time, the emptiness wasn't resignation; it was a chilling calm, the calm before the storm. It was the eye of the hurricane, the silence before the fury she was about to unleash.

Her past—woven from betrayal and loss—still clung to her like the scent of woodsmoke, a constant reminder of the life stolen from her, of the trust shattered beyond repair. But she wasn't broken. She was a crucible forged in the fires of grief, tempered by a steely resolve. She was a hunter. Justice wouldn't wait, and neither would she.

The rain lashed against her skin, icy needles mirroring the icy determination in her eyes. The stolen SUV growled to life under her touch. Then the earth shuddered. The warehouse, a concrete mausoleum of her past, erupted in a blinding inferno. The night sky, ripped open by a monstrous fireball, illuminated the landscape in a hellish light, the flash brighter than the lightning storm that filled the sky. The roar was deafening—the sound of judgment delivered.

Delia didn't flinch. Her gaze, fixed on the road ahead, was unwavering. The rain, now a torrent, cascaded off the SUV, obscuring the fiery wreckage behind her. She drove towards her destiny, a lone figure swallowed by the storm, The future was a knife-edge, but she would walk it, head held high, forged anew in the flames of her revenge.

| 33 |

A Fragile Alliance

Elena stood at the kitchen window, her phone to her ear. She was watching Thorne, who was standing at the edge of the cliff looking out over the ocean. The phone was answered.

"Where the hell have you been?" asked the voice on the other end of the call. The voice was cold and unemotional, with a hint of a foreign accent. A voice that could send chills down your spine.

"I've got Thorne with me. I need your help," said Elena.

"What do you need?" the voice asked.

Elena was silent for a few seconds. She needed to be careful about how she talked about what she needed. She was on a knife-edge with this client, and she was concerned that they may decide to handle this without her help.

"Thorne's life is in danger," she said. "We're in a safe house right now, but it won't be long until someone finds us. She may be on her way here right now. We need to get Thorne out of the country, but I'm concerned that his private jet may be under surveillance."

"Does he have the product?" asked the voice.

"I am working on getting the access codes, but he's keeping them close to the chest."

The voice was quiet. She could hear him breathing. It sounded like he was trying to calm his voice before speaking again.

"The director is dead," said the voice.

Elena was stunned. She raised her hand to her mouth.

"That can't be. I had lunch with him at his club the day before yesterday. Everything was arranged."

"Whatever you arranged is no longer," said the voice. "You have failed your assignment. We want Thorne, and we want the codes. You are expendable."

Elena was taken aback by the steel in his voice. "There are circumstances . . ."

"Your job, the reason we hired you, was to deal with circumstances. You assured us you could handle the circumstances. Now we hear another assassin has gotten involved. Deal with it, and then we will talk." The line went dead, and she stared at the phone.

"Fucking Delia. This is all her fault."

Elena's mind raced as she processed the abrupt termination of the call. She knew her position was precarious and that the news of the director's demise would add to the urgency of her situation. As Thorne approached the house, she felt a surge of determination. She would need to act decisively to secure Thorne's cooperation and ensure their escape. Every second counted. Elena steeled herself as she prepared to confront Thorne. She knew that gaining access to the codes was crucial, but she also needed to keep Thorne's trust. Their lives depended on it.

As Thorne entered the house, Elena's heart raced. She knew that the next few moments would shape their fate.

"Thorne," she said, her voice steady despite the turmoil within. "We need to leave now. Our safe house may be compromised, and your life is in grave danger. I need your cooperation. We must retrieve the access codes and get you to a secure location."

Thorne slumped into the chair and rested his arms on the table. "Those fucking codes," he said, his voice low and pitiful. "I wish I had never created the app. It's done nothing but ruin my life."

Elena had never seen him like this. His face was ashen, and he had tears in his eyes. She sat in the chair next to him. "We can make everything all right," she said, placing her hand on his arm. "My client is still interested. We can make the deal, take the money and disappear. No one will ever find us."

He raised his head and looked at her. "Yeah. As long as I provide the codes."

Peters, the remaining security guard, sauntered into the kitchen, his face showing the weariness they were all feeling. "Anyone seen Jefferson? I can't find him anywhere."

Elena looked up at him. "I had coffee with him this morning, but now that you mention it, I haven't seen him all day."

She saw the concern spread across his face. Thorne looked up from the table. "Have we been compromised?" he asked.

"I'll check the front of the property," said Elena. "Peters, check the back along the cliff. If he's hiding, that's the perfect place."

Elena headed towards the front door, and Peters, pulling his pistol from his shoulder holster, stepped through the back door and headed towards the cliffs. Thorne sat at the table and smiled. This was all working out perfectly. Elena thought she had him running scared so he would drop everything and get the codes. He wondered what her next move would be.

As Peters disappeared through the back door, Elena stepped onto the front porch. The sun was setting, casting an orange hue over the ocean, and she squinted into the fading light, searching for any signs of movement. She moved off the porch, silenced pistol in hand, and made her way around the house to the edge of the property. She spotted Peters walking along the cliff, looking down at the small sliver of beach that was exposed at low tide. She walked towards Peters, her pistol behind her back. As she approached, Peters turned to face her.

"Anything?" she asked.

Peters had sensed something, and he was prepared, but not prepared enough. Elena's pistol appeared in a flash, and she pulled the trigger twice before he could react. He flew off the cliff to the rocks and surf below. Elena stepped to the edge as the sun fell behind the ocean. She looked over in the fading light and saw Peters splattered on the rocks below. As soon as the tide changed, he would disappear into oblivion, just like Jefferson.

Elena's hand tightened around the phone in her pocket, a reminder of the harsh reality of her situation. Failure was not an option, and she would need to use all her skills to navigate the challenges that lay ahead. Getting rid of Peters was the last piece of the puzzle. Now all she needed to do was convince Thorne to get the codes and she could call her client and arrange an extraction.

She decided on a different approach. She had tried fear, but it made Thorne more resistant. It was time to try something else. Something more seductive.

Meanwhile, Thorne remained at the table, his eyes darting back and forth as he plotted his next move. He knew that Elena's client was growing impatient, and the promise of the access codes was his only bargaining chip.

"I need to play this just right," he muttered to himself. "Elena thinks she has me figured out, but she doesn't know the half of it." His mind flashed back to the creation of the app and the secrets it held—secrets that could change everything.

| 34 |

The New Approach

Elena, lying naked on the bed, regarded Thorne with a mixture of suspicion and grudging admiration. Their unlikely alliance had been forged in the fires of a shared threat, spun by the very organization that had once been Elena's lifeblood. The ocean breeze cooled by the rain made her skin tingle and her nipples hard. They had made love with a passion that neither had felt in a long time. Maybe the threat of death made their lovemaking more urgent, or maybe the things Elena did to Thorne's body had turned him into putty in her hands. Hands that knew how to please.

Thorne, his face etched with the weight of his own secrets, looked at her. She was gorgeous, her red hair draped around her porcelain face like a fiery halo. She had done things to him that made his entire body scream for more, and she had delivered. Now sated, for the first time in the last couple of days, he felt safe. He knew Elena had his back inside the house while Peters protected the outside.

He knew little about Elena. She had entered his life when he seemed to need something other than his programming.

He had witnessed her capabilities firsthand, the cold precision with which she had dispatched his own security detail, the way her eyes, warm and captivating, hardened into ice when she was in the zone.

"We need to be cautious," Elena said, her voice low, her gaze unwavering. "They're relentless. They'll stop at nothing to get what they want. My clients are ready to make a move now. They will protect you and me at all costs. You need to decide. You remained hidden for years.

Where we are going, no one will ever find us."

"I disappeared to protect what I created," Thorne explained, his voice taking on a raw edge. "To shield my work from those who would use it for their own twisted ends."

"You can't trust the Americans," Delia said, her voice laced with a raw emotion that Thorne had never heard before. "They're a plague, spreading across the world, leaving devastation in their wake."

"And your client. How are they different?" Thorne asked.

"My clients are a consortium, not a country. They will use your app to bring communications and education to the parts of the world where that is not possible. They will bring your dream to fruition, on a huge scale."

Elena couldn't care less about either situation. She would be rich beyond her wildest dreams, and Thorne would be dead or in prison in some godforsaken country where no one would ever find him.

Elena knew they had to work together to fight the darkness that threatened to engulf them both. But trust was a fragile thing, a delicate thread that could easily be broken.

She had to tread carefully, each step a gamble, each move a reasoned risk.

They were a fragile alliance, a paradox of light and darkness, drawn together by the forces of fate. She had set this up so they had no choice but to trust each other, to gamble on the possibility that their shared goal, the salvation of the world, might be the one thing that could bind them together.

"I will not let them destroy everything," Elena said, her voice filled with a newfound conviction. "Not the world, not you, not me."

Thorne nodded. "Then tomorrow we will call your client and sell them Nexus. I will have the codes by the end of the day."

His eyes met hers, reflecting the fire that burned in her heart. He embraced her, and the kiss was wet and eager. She reached under the sheets and felt him grow in her hand. She broke from the kiss and slid under the sheets, her lips traveling down his body. Thorne was all hers.

| 35 |

Journey Towards Death

The rain hammered the windshield, a relentless percussion against the slick black ribbon unspooling before her. Delia gripped the wheel, knuckles bone white, the scent of ozone and wet asphalt stinging her nostrils. Each swipe of the wipers was a frantic heartbeat against the suffocating silence of the predawn. The low hills to the east bled a bruised purple as the clouds broke, mirroring the turmoil in her gut. Elena had to die. That was the cold, brutal truth. But Thorne . . . the ache in her chest tightened. His impossible dreams of a better world, his eyes that held the vast, star-dusted hope of a dying galaxy. Could she extinguish that light?

Her decision, made before the infernal journey began, felt like a brand seared into her soul. Thorne. A sacrifice at the altar of her marriage—a marriage to David, the solid earth beneath her feet, the man who treated her like a queen, his touch a balm against the festering wounds of her life. David: her future, her rock.

But Thorne's creation . . . that monstrous app, a digital Pandora's box . . . it gnawed at her. The thought of its release, the chilling prospect of unleashing its power into the world, clawed at her throat. Every nation, every terrorist cell, armed with a weapon capable of unimaginable chaos. Open source? A digital plague sweeping the globe. The alternative was just as horrifying: a sale to some shadowy cabal, its potential for devastation equally monstrous.

The bile rose in her throat. There was no other choice. She had to destroy it. Even if it meant sacrificing Thorne. The app had to be erased, every line of code annihilated before it could corrupt the world, before it could consume everything she held dear. The weight of the world, the blood-soaked responsibility, pressed down on her, suffocating her in the claustrophobic darkness of the approaching dawn.

Delia checked the nav system. Her destination lay thirty minutes ahead. She needed to prepare herself for what was to come. She had no idea how large a security force Elena had put together to protect Thorne. She didn't even know if they were at the house. For all she knew, they could be hundreds or thousands of miles away, the program already in the hands of the highest bidder. She needed to stay positive. She still had time, but she needed closure on this nightmare she had been living.

She spotted a sign ahead and pulled into the small diner, a parking lot full of pickup trucks. She stopped the SUV, put her hair up under her hat, slid out of the SUV and put on a nylon windbreaker. She felt to make sure her knives were in place and that her pistol would be accessible if need be. She closed the door and walked to the entrance.

The smell of bacon was overpowering as she pushed open the door. Conversation seemed to stop as she entered the space and found an open booth near the window. Delia slid into the booth, the eyes of the diner's patrons heavy on her. She kept her head down, her hat pulled low, and avoided eye contact. The bacon smell was overwhelming, greasy, and she felt a twist of nausea as she realized she hadn't eaten since the previous morning. She needed to keep her strength up, especially if things were about to get messy.

Ordering a coffee, a stack of pancakes and bacon, she took a moment to gather herself, her hands trembling as she wrapped them around the warm mug. Her mind raced with the possibilities of what lay ahead. Thorne, Elena, the app—they were all interconnected pieces in this deadly puzzle.

As she ate, she went over her plan, her thoughts drifting to David, her steadfast anchor in this turbulent sea. He was her calm amidst the chaos, and the thought of him steadied her resolve. She knew the lives that hung in the balance, but she couldn't shake the certainty that this was the only way. The alternative—a world ravaged by Thorne's creation—was unthinkable.

Finishing her meal, she left a generous tip, a paltry attempt to pay forward some kindness in a world that felt devoid of it. As she stepped back out into the rain, the cool droplets felt like a baptism, washing away her hesitation and solidifying her purpose.

A sense of foreboding washed over her. She pulled her jacket closer, a futile attempt to shield herself from the elements and the weight of her choices. Thorne, with his idealistic dreams, and David, her steadfast rock—their faces flashed in her mind, a stark reminder of the duel between hope and practicality.

The diner loomed behind her, its warm glow a stark contrast to the gloomy sky. She knew that once she left, there was no turning back. The nav system ticked down the minutes to her destination, each second a reminder of the time bomb that was Thorne's app. Delia's hands tightened on the wheel, her knuckles whitening once more.

The rain intensified, as if the heavens themselves were weeping for the choices she had to make. In her mind, she saw Elena's face, a mixture of determination and greed, and knew that her decision was the only way to prevent a digital Armageddon. The world was teetering on the edge, and she had to be the one to pull it back.

As she approached the house, a sense of unease settled in the pit of her stomach. The security measures were unknown, and the possibility of failure loomed large. But she had come too far to turn back now. With a steady hand, she drew her pistol, a familiar weight that offered little comfort. Step by step, she moved, her breath steady despite the turmoil within. The rain-soaked world awaited its fate, and Delia knew that her actions in the next few moments would shape not just her destiny but that of humanity itself.

| 36 |

Trust in Question

Thorne watched Elena with an intensity that made her skin prickle. His eyes, a deep, fathomless green, seemed to see right through her, reading every thought, every fear she carried in the shadows of her mind.

"You have to understand," he said, his voice a low rumble that resonated in the modest bedroom of the beach house. "I can't just hand over my creation to them. It's too dangerous.

"They want to control it," he continued, his voice laced with a palpable urgency, "to weaponize it. They don't care about the consequences. All they care about is the power, the potential for domination."

Elena had heard it all before. It was the same logic that had driven her client to offer several billion dollars in gold to own the program, the same twisted ambition that fueled their deadly conflict. But there was something different here, something she couldn't quite define. It wasn't just his vulnerability, the desperation in his voice. It was the conviction in his eyes, his unwavering belief that he was on the right side of this fight.

"So what do you suggest?" she asked, covering her naked body with a sheet. Her voice was clipped and controlled, even as the warmth of his gaze chipped away at the icy armor she wore. "Last night, you promised me you would sell the program to my client. What changed now?"

"Your client made an incredibly generous offer, but I am concerned they will not use the program for the good I intended. I need to be sure of their intentions."

"What does that mean?" she asked, confused.

He laughed and ran his hand over her breast, toying with her nipple. "Tell your client I want ten billion dollars, and they have twenty-four hours to comply or I will release it as open source."

His words hung in the air, a daring proposition that felt dangerous and exhilarating all at once. It was a gamble, a leap of faith, and she was caught in the cross fire of her emotions. She stared at him in disbelief. So this was what his scruples cost.

"That's twice what they offered. I don't know if I can sell it. What makes you think they will trust you not to open-source it anyway?" she challenged, her voice sharper than she intended. "What makes you think I can risk my life, my own principles?"

His gaze held hers, unwavering. "Because," he said, his voice low and intense, "your job is to deliver the program and me."

Elena was stunned. "What are you talking about? I'm just the intermediary, trying to work a deal. Nothing else."

He laughed and twisted her hard nipple. "You're an assassin. Your job was to make sure I did what your client wants or to kill me, whatever works best. You're someone who understands the price of power and the consequences of its misuse."

She squealed and pulled away. This was a side of Thorne she hadn't seen before. He was right, of course, but she had never been one to jeopardize her mission, to let personal feelings interfere with her duty.

"This is a dangerous game you're playing," she said, her voice laced with a newfound hesitation. "that could end in disaster for both of us."

He nodded, his expression grim. "I know. But it's a game I have to play, a fight I have to win. And I need you to convince your client that I'm serious."

The air thickened further, the silence between them heavy. Her mind raced, trying to weigh the risks, to find a path through the treacherous maze. She had always lived in the shadows, a master of manipulation and deception, and here she was, being manipulated by a common computer programmer—well, maybe not common.

"I need time," she said, her voice a whisper, a plea that echoed in the vast silence of the room.

He nodded, his gaze softening. "Don't wait too long. This deal has an expiration date."

His words echoed in her head as she questioned how long she had been played. She was caught in a labyrinth where the stakes were higher than ever before. She felt like a chess piece, moved across the board by unseen forces, each move a step towards a predetermined end.

But she felt like a pawn when she was supposed to be a player, a force to be reckoned with. It now appeared that Thorne was more devious than she had been led to believe.

Elena slipped out from under the covers, put on a pair of sweatpants and a sweatshirt and grabbed her phone. She stepped out of the room and dialed a number.

"Is there a problem?" asked the voice on the phone. "The target's technology poses a significant threat to our operations."

"He wants ten billion in gold," said Elena.

The voice laughed. "So, our little do-gooder can be bought. That's more than we authorized you to offer. What happened?"

Elena looked at her reflection in the window. She looked tired. "I think he has been playing me all along. He says he will open-source the program in twenty-four hours if you don't agree."

"So the great Elena Petrova has been played. You are human. Who would have guessed?"

He laughed, and the call disconnected. His words were a slap in the face, but something within her had shifted, a spark of defiance ignited by her client's words.

Elena walked back to the bedroom. Thorne was sitting against the headboard. "Well. Do we have a deal?" "They're working on it. It will take time."

"Time they don't have," said Thorne.

Elena stopped walking towards the bed and stared out the open patio door. A tickle ran up her spine. Her internal warning system. She looked at Thorne. "Get dressed, quickly."

She reached under the mattress and pulled out two pistols and a stiletto. Thorne's eyes grew wide. He threw off the covers and slipped into a pair of jeans.

"What the fuck?" he asked.

"I don't think my client was in the mood to wait for you to make up your mind."

"How did they find us, and where the hell is Peters?"

"Peters is at the bottom of the cliff," she said. "We need to move."

She held up one pistol. "Do you know how to use this?" Thorne nodded. Elena threw the gun onto the bed and turned off the light. She headed for the kitchen, Thorne hot on her tail. She pointed towards the couch in the living room.

"Get behind there and shoot anyone who isn't me."

"Where are you going?" he asked, but she was already moving out the back door. He heard the first bullets hit the wall, and the kitchen window exploded.

| 37 |

A Dangerous Gamble

Delia moved through the trees surrounding the rural home overlooking the Pacific Ocean. She wasn't certain she had the right property until she spotted several shadowy figures moving through the trees ahead of her. She pulled her pistol as she reached the tree line and got her first view of the nondescript house. The sound of suppressed rifle fire filled the night, and she heard bullets slam into the wood siding of the house and glass shattering.

Delia, with her pistol drawn, skirted the property until she was looking at the back side of the home. She had just ducked behind a pine tree when a black-clad ninja, wearing a balaclava to hide his face, crawled through the undergrowth and took up a position where he had a straight bead on the house. She slipped around him, placed the tip of her silenced pistol an inch from the back of his head and pulled the trigger. His body bounced as death took him to his final resting place. More movement beyond the trees caught her attention. She moved across the open yard, crouched as low as she could go.

As she moved, she took out another ninja crawling across the rough grass. She looked up as the back door opened and a barefoot woman dressed in sweats ran from the house. She dropped two ninjas coming around the side of the house and dove for cover as the surrounding walls exploded in wood chips.

Elena. Even in the dark, she would have known it was Elena. She moved the same way Delia did. The same movements, the same speed and accuracy. For Delia, it was like watching herself in action. Bullets were slamming into the house as Elena returned fire.

"If Elena is covering the back of the house, who's covering the front, and where's Thorne?" she asked to herself.

Delia raced back towards the tree line, dropping another ninja as he rose from a spot behind a large tree. She never stopped moving. Rounding the front corner, she spotted four dark figures approaching the front door in a diamond formation. She didn't hesitate. She ran towards the four figures and fired four times. All the dark figures dropped to the ground, one of them getting off a shot that sliced a gash in her arm. She switched hands and placed a round in his head. She walked over and shot each person in the head as they lay on the ground. She reloaded and approached the front door. Several bullets slammed into the door and the frame, showering her with wood chips. She reared back and kicked the door just below the lockset. The door flew open, and she dove into the house, flipping over and kicking the door shut.

A shot rang out and slammed into the wall next to her.

"Thorne, is that you behind the couch?"

"Delia?" a voice said nervously as more bullets slammed into the house and the door. Thorne looked up from behind the couch. "They're onto me, Delia," he said. "They're going to kill me and Elena. You have to save me."

Delia's heart hammered against her ribs. This was it. She had known this day would come, but the reality of it was far more terrifying than she had imagined.

"Who's coming for you, Thorne?" Delia asked, her voice a steady whisper, a stark contrast to the storm raging inside her.

"I won't let them have it, Delia," Thorne said, his eyes burning with a fierce determination. "I'll fight them. But I need your help. They're too strong. I can't do this alone."

"What did you do, Thorne?" she asked as she heard movement behind the door; she fired four shots into the door. She heard a grunt as a body hit the floor of the front porch.

"I offered to sell Nexus to Elena's client, then I upped the price. I guess they didn't like it. Save me, Delia, and I will give you half. You'll be rich. Over two billion dollars. Just get me out of here." He was scared.

A bullet slammed into his shoulder, and he flew from behind the couch. Delia dropped a dark figure coming down the bedroom hall.

"Thorne. What about Elena?"

Thorne, losing blood, looked at Delia. "She was just using me. Get me out of here and we'll get the codes ourselves. You know where they are. She brought this all on herself. To hell with her."

Delia knew Thorne was lying. She could read it on his face.

"Thorne, what was the plan after you sold the codes to Elena's client?"

"That's the beauty of my plan. Once I got their money and moved it to various safe locations, I was going to release the code as an open-source program. They would have been fucked. Delia, I fell in love with you the first time I saw you. I want us to be together forever."

Delia heard movement at the back of the house. She grabbed Thorne's good arm. "We need to move. We're being boxed in," she said.

She dragged Thorne out of the living room and into the kitchen. She looked at the pathetic piece of humanity that stood before her, with his bloody shoulder, and she saw the deceit in his face. Thorne had sold out his principles for money and was going to screw over the people he sold it to, most likely the same people who were now trying to kill him. She was disgusted. She raised her pistol and pointed it at his chest. Thorne stared at the pistol.

"I believed you were different, that you wanted to change the world. It turns out you are like all the rest, a conniving little shit with no morals or principles." Her finger moved to the trigger.

A blast of machine-gun fire came through the kitchen window. Thorne took the brunt of it, bullets riddling his body. Delia shoved Thorne and fired through the broken glass. A body hit the ground with a thud. She reached down to her side and her hand came away covered in blood. She slid over and checked Thorne. No pulse.

Delia slipped back into the living room as two figures entered from the hall. She grabbed her knives and flipped both of them. Her aim was spot-on, and both figures gurgled as blood exploded from their throats. She holstered her pistol and picked up the two assault rifles the figures were carrying. She checked the magazine and headed for the bedroom.

"This ends now," she said to herself.

Delia charged through the bedroom doors and out onto the deck. She fired across the lawn and took out two more dark figures. She jumped off the deck, landed on her feet and raced across the lawn, firing at anything that moved.

She emptied both rifles and dropped them onto the lawn, pulled her pistol and continued the fight. As she ran onto the patio, she stopped and listened. There was no more gunfire coming from around the house.

Delia reloaded her pistol and stepped off the patio. There were dead bodies all over the lawn. She walked around, shooting anyone that was still moving. She spotted a lump moving near the cliff and walked towards it. Elena was covered in blood, her left arm hanging limp at her side and blood pooled next to her. Delia stopped. Elena looked up at her, blood covering her face.

She smiled a pained smile. "Bet you never thought you'd see me again. Huh?"

"I thought you were dead," said Delia. "How?"

Elena coughed, blood dripping from her mouth.

"Next time, take the head shot. I guess it wasn't my time to go. You didn't have to shoot me. I would have shared the scroll with you. I loved you, Delia, like I loved no one before or since. We had something wonderful. Something I will always cherish."

Elena's hand moved with lightning speed, but Delia was faster, and the bullet crashed into Elena's head. She flopped back onto the ground, the pistol falling next to her. Delia walked over to the body and stared down at it.

"I loved you too, Elena. More than anyone before or since." She smiled. "This time I took the head shot."

She pushed the body with her foot, and it rolled off the cliff and slammed into the rocks below. Within seconds, the waves pulled it from the rocks and carried it out to sea. She walked back to the house and entered the living room. Thorne's body lay on the floor, riddled with bullet holes.

She looked down at him.

"You could have had everything," she said, with no emotion in her voice. "I would have protected you."

Delia heard sirens screaming in the distance and walked out the kitchen door to the tree line. She looked back at the house and the carnage and headed for her SUV. Her nightmare was over, but someone else's was just beginning.

| 38 |

Reckoning with the Past

The chill of the hospital room wrapped around her like a shroud, the sterile white walls amplifying the silence, echoing the hollowness she felt inside. The scent of antiseptic brought a wave of nausea. Her reflection in the frosted glass of the window was a stranger, her eyes hollowed, her skin drained of its usual vibrancy.

She had made the impossible choice, sacrificing the man she had once admired to save the world from the chaos he could have unleashed. Her decision had been a gut-wrenching one, a betrayal of her own heart and a desperate act of self-preservation. In the end, she had chosen the mission over the man, duty. She had survived. She had emerged from the fire, scarred but alive. The price of her survival was etched upon her soul, a permanent reminder of the sacrifices she had made. The world was safe, for now, but the victory felt hollow, bitter and tainted by grief.

She had to go on the run—a fugitive, a shadow flitting through the night. The Organization would be after her, their trust shattered, their wrath burning. They saw her as a traitor, a liability, a rogue agent. They had stripped her of her identity, her past, her future, leaving her with nothing but the scars of her choices.

The shadows that had consumed her for so long were now etched upon her soul, an undeniable presence that she could not escape. They whispered secrets, revealed truths she had hidden from herself and forced her to confront her own darkness.

She had always been a warrior, a hunter, a silent executioner. She had lived in a world of shadows and subterfuge, where emotions were a liability and attachments a weakness. She had honed her skills with precision, mastering the art of deception, becoming one with the night. But in that moment, staring at her own reflection in the cold, sterile window, she knew something had changed.

She was no longer the cold, calculating assassin she had once been. She was a woman broken, wounded and haunted by her past. The memories flooded back, each one a searing reminder of the path she had chosen, the sacrifices she had made, the lives she had taken. She saw the faces of her victims, their eyes staring back at her, accusing, judging. Their pain was a tangible presence, a constant ache in her soul. She had been trained to suppress her emotions, to detach herself from the consequences of her actions, but now, in the quiet of the hospital room, she could no longer ignore the truth.

She had become a monster, a weapon forged in the crucible of violence and deceit. She had tasted the bitterness of power, the seductive allure of control. And now she was paying the price, the price of her choices, the price of her betrayal.

Her heart ached with longing for a life she could never have, a life filled with sunshine and laughter, a life where love was not a liability but a blessing. Her world was a world of darkness, where shadows formed and secrets whispered. And now she was being pulled back into that world, its clutches tightening around her, its darkness threatening to consume her. She had to escape, to break free from the shackles of her past and find redemption. She needed to forgive herself, to accept the consequences of her choices, to find a path to a future where she could be something more than a shadow of her former self.

The sound of a gentle knock on the door startled her, and she opened her eyes, trying to focus. She turned to see a woman in a white coat; her face was kind, her eyes filled with compassion.

"Hi," she said, her voice soft, "you're awake."

She nodded, her throat dry and scratchy. "Where am I?" she croaked, her voice a whisper.

"You're in a private hospital," she replied, her smile reassuring. "You were injured in a firefight. You went to someone for help after you were injured, and they brought you to me, but you're going to be all right. You're safe."

Injured in a firefight. The memories came rushing back—fragments of chaos and violence, the searing pain in her side, the deafening roar of gunfire. The attack. The betrayal. The man who died at her feet. The man she had intended to kill.

Delia's fearful eyes locked onto the woman's. The doctor smiled and stepped closer to the bed.

"Rest easy. We do not know your name, and there is no record of you ever having been treated here. No one will find you here."

Delia closed her eyes but amidst the darkness, a flicker of hope remained. A faint ember of determination refused to die. She had to live, to heal and to make things right. For herself, for David and for the world she had sworn to protect.

The doctor squeezed her hand, her touch warm and reassuring. "You're strong," she whispered. "You have faced unimaginable challenges, and you have survived. You will find your way, and you will find what you are looking for."

Her words were a balm to Delia's wounded soul. They offered her a glimmer of hope in the face of despair, a promise of a future that was not yet lost. She closed her eyes, taking a deep breath, allowing the warmth of the words to wash over her. She was going to be okay. She was going to find her way back. She was going to find redemption. And she was going to get revenge.

| 39 |

A Changed Woman

The sterile white walls of the hospital room seemed to press in on her, a stark contrast to the vibrant life she'd once known. It was a life she never wanted to return to, but it was the life she knew. Her body was healing, the scars fading, but her mind was still reeling from the whirlwind of events that had unfolded. The last few days felt like a fever dream, a blur of action, betrayal and an unexpected love that had shattered her world, a world that was now fractured, replaced by something raw and unpredictable.

The conflict had reached a fever pitch, a crescendo of emotions and actions. She had been forced to make a decision that would alter the course of her life. The world hung in the balance, its fate resting on her shoulders. In the end, she had chosen the right course. It was a risky choice, a dangerous leap of faith. But it was a choice born of conviction, of a belief that Thorne could be a force for good, a force capable of overcoming even the darkest of shadows. She was wrong.

She had survived the fight, but the victory came at a price. The battle had left her wounded, scarred both physically and emotionally. She had lost a part of herself, a part that had defined her existence for so long. As she sat in the sterile white room, she reflected on her journey.

The world was a different place now. The threat of global chaos had been averted, but the scars of the battle were still etched deep within her. Her life had been changed, the woman she once was a distant memory, a spirit in the rearview mirror.

The woman who emerged from the wreckage was different, stronger, more aware of the fragility of life and the power of possibility. She had found a sliver of hope in the darkest of places; she was a woman who had learned the true meaning of sacrifice. The road forward was uncertain, the future full of unknowns. She had chosen a new path, one where love, not duty, would guide her choices.

Thorne was gone. He had become a symbol of hope, a beacon of light in a world consumed by darkness. But in the end, the power he held consumed him, his compassion and longing for a better future run over by the evil that drained him.

Delia's journey was not over. The scars were a reminder of the battles she had fought, the sacrifices she had made. But they were also a reminder of the woman she had become, who had dared to embrace her vulnerability, had chosen love over duty. Delia was ready to face whatever the future held.

The world was a fragile place, and she had learned that even the smallest act of kindness, the smallest act of love, could make a difference. And that was enough. That was all she needed to embrace the new dawn that was breaking over the horizon.

| 40 |

The Enemy Within

The lights in the apartment remained off. Delia lay in the bed sipping from her glass of wine. The doctor had patched her up, and she was now resting comfortably. Her heart pounded against her ribs. The shadows from the lights outside moved across the ceiling. Her mission had reached its climax. Every muscle in her body was taut. Everything hurt. But she knew her job wasn't finished.

The clock ticked relentlessly, each second echoing the weight of the world resting on her shoulders. The billionaire, a man she saw as both a danger and a fascination, was no longer a threat. He had been destroyed because he couldn't decide what was more important to him.

Delia slid out of the bed and dressed. She had spent these past couple of days thinking about those final moments and the last words Thorne had spoken to her.

"You know where it is," he'd said.

She'd thought about it long and hard, and then earlier this morning it had come to her like a dream. "Is it possible?"

Delia placed her knives in her boots and holstered her pistol. She needed to see if she was right, even though she knew it was still dangerous. People were still looking for Thorne's program.

Thorne's penthouse, a fortress of glass and steel, was her destination. The operation was perfectly orchestrated. She knew what she needed to do, her actions synchronized in her head. But as she infiltrated the building, a disquieting sense of unease settled over Delia. She knew the FBI, who were investigating the actions that had taken place at the beach house, had cordoned the building off. As part of that investigation, there was a team covering his mansion and the penthouse, although she knew that the real purpose was to find the program.

Delia looked in the mirror. Her gorgeous blond hair was now fiery red and cut short, hanging just to her neck. She was stunned by how much she looked like Elena. They could have been sisters. She hung the FBI ID lanyard around her neck and clipped the badge to her belt. It was one of her many disguises. One last look in the mirror, and she left the apartment.

Delia slid under the crime-scene tape and entered the lobby. Instead of a security guard, the desk was now manned by two FBI agents. She approached the desk and held up her ID. She knew that presenting herself with authority would be the difference between getting into the building or dying here in the lobby.

"Who are you?" the taller agent asked, his hand instinctively reaching for his weapon.

Delia smiled. "McCarthy, counterterrorism. Who's left upstairs?" she asked, speaking with authority.

The agent looked at a clipboard sitting on the desk.

"Looks like just about everyone's left. You need to go up?"

"Yes," said Delia. "Just need to follow up on a few things."

"What things?" asked the second agent.

Delia stared at him. "That's need to know, and you don't need to know." Her hand rested on the butt of her pistol.

The agent sneered and slid the clipboard over to her, and Delia signed in. She thanked the agent and headed for the elevator. She was relieved that she didn't have to kill them. Yet.

Delia stepped off the elevator and looked at the blood-stains on the marble floor, not quite dried. She stepped around them and entered the art vault. She needed to be sure she understood Thorne's last words.

The vault door was still lying in pieces on the floor. She entered the room, leaving the lights off, and made her way to the painting. Her heart skipped a beat when she saw it hanging on the wall. She turned on her flashlight and stood for a minute, looking at it. There was nothing exceptional about it, just a pretty oil painting done a long time ago by Thorne's mother.

Delia stood and listened. Hearing no noise, she reached over and pulled the painting from the wall. She held her breath as she turned the painting over.

Delia smiled as she removed the black plastic bag that was taped to the back of the painting. She hung the painting back on the wall and opened the bag. The black external hard drive was there, just like in her dream. Thorne had known that if she had found her way to the beach house, she would have been able to find the small package. She closed the bag and placed it in the pocket of her jacket.

A noise behind her startled her, and she turned. A woman, short and pretty, wearing an FBI windbreaker, stood at the door. She had her hand on the backstrap of her pistol, still in her hip holster. Delia turned and faced the woman. She held up her ID.

"I was following up on a few things, and since I was here, my partner had told me about all the art pieces he had seen. Thought I'd check them out for myself. Didn't mean to intrude." She smiled at the female agent and walked towards the vault door. The agent backed up a few feet.

"I need to see your ID," said the agent. Delia removed the ID from her neck, and it fell to the floor.

"Sorry," she said. She kneeled to pick up the ID and removed the knife from her boot. She stood, stepped toward the agent and handed her the ID. The agent took it and looked at the digital notebook she was holding.

"I just need to check this," she said.

She looked at the ID and typed on the notepad. She waited for what seemed like an eternity, then a strange look crossed her face and she lowered the notepad as she reached for her pistol. Delia's knife flew and penetrated the agent's throat. She grabbed her throat and fell to her knees, disbelief in her eyes. Delia stepped closer, avoiding the blood spatter, grabbed the knife and slid it across the agent's throat, completing the job. She removed the knife, wiped the blood off on the agent's sleeve and placed the knife back in her boot.

She dragged the agent into the art vault and tucked her body behind a large shipping crate. Delia looked around to make sure there was no one else there, picked up the notepad and looked at the screen. NO

ID MATCH appeared in big letters on the screen. She threw the notepad into the vault and headed for the elevator.

Delia exited the elevator, walked to the counter and signed out. She thanked the agents and walked towards the door. Just as she reached the door, the taller agent called out.

"Hey, McCarthy."

Delia froze, her hand reaching towards her weapon. She turned her head.

"Wanna get a drink sometime?"

She relaxed and smiled at the agent. "Call me sometime. I'm in the directory."

The agent smiled, and Delia stepped through the door and disappeared into the night.

| 41 |

The Price of Freedom

When word of Thorne's death was reported, world governments and their intelligence agencies breathed a collective sigh of relief mixed with trepidation. The crisis had been averted, the threat neutralized, but the scars remained. The app, the insidious creation of a man Delia loved, was gone, but its potential for chaos was not yet extinguished. The echoes of its power reverberated, a reminder of the fragility of peace and the need to locate the codes and make sure they were secure.

The international community scrambled to assess the damage, the fallout from a near miss that had brought humanity to the brink. Governments, once embroiled in a tangled web of mistrust, now sought common ground, realizing the shared threat they faced. Thorne's death and the location of the program were shrouded in mystery, leaving a void that amplified the anxieties of nations.

Delia stood at the start of a new world. Her actions, had reshaped the geopolitical landscape. The price of freedom had been steep, a burden she carried with a heavy heart.

The Organization, her shadowy employer, was fractured, its power diminished by the events that had unfolded. That trust, once unwavering, had crumbled, leaving a void of uncertainty in its wake.

Delia's identity, once so compartmentalized, was now a mosaic of contradictions. She was the assassin who had saved the world from a catastrophe, yet she bore the weight of the lives she had taken, the sacrifices demanded by her profession. She was the woman who had fallen in love, her heart yearning for a future she would never have, a love entwined with the memory of Thorne's death.

She wandered the streets of her city, a spectre in her own life. The familiar routines, the normalcy she had once embraced now seemed distant, a fading memory. Her world was a jumble of shattered expectations, a canvas painted with shades of grief and uncertainty. The shadows of her past, the weight of her choices, clung to her like a shroud, reminding her of the cost of her actions.

In the crisis's aftermath, the world grappled with its own demons. Thorne's app, had exposed the vulnerability of the global order. The threat of cyber warfare, once a distant specter, now loomed large, a tangible danger in a world where technology held unprecedented power.

Nations, shaken by the would move to pour massive resources into cybersecurity, investing in sophisticated defenses to protect their critical infrastructure. Treaties would be forged, international collaborations established, a united front against a new breed of adversaries. The crisis had served as a stark reminder, a catalyst for a new era of global cooperation, albeit forged in the crucible of fear.

Delia, however, found little solace in the world's new-found unity. Global attention had shifted to the threat of cyberwar, but she knew that the true threat lay not in technology but in the darkness that dwelled within the human heart. Thorne's creation reflected the human capacity for both brilliance and depravity, a reminder that even the most noble inventions could be twisted into weapons of destruction.

Her thoughts turned to the man she had chosen to protect, the enigmatic billionaire whose death weighed on her mind. He had been a puzzle she had yearned to solve, a man of contradictions, a brilliant mind consumed by shadows. His absence, a hole in her life, fueled a constant questioning, an unrelenting search for answers.

Now he was gone, swallowed by the very shadows he had sought to escape. His death, a cruel twist of fate, had left her with a feeling of betrayal and a yearning for answers that might never come.

The questions lingered, a persistent ache in her soul. She had saved the world and protected it from the havoc the billionaire's app could wreak. But in doing so, she had sacrificed the man, a loss as immense as the consequences she had averted.

The price of freedom was a heavy one, a burden she bore with a quiet dignity. The world had been saved, but at a profound cost. As she walked through the city, a lone figure hiding in the shadows, she knew that her life would never be the same. The echoes of the crisis, the scars of her choices, would haunt her, a constant reminder of the price she had paid for a world that was free from the threat of nuclear annihilation.

The consequences of her decision, the sacrifice she had made, had forged a new resolve within her. She had experienced the bitterness of loss, the pain of betrayal, the fragility of life. And yet, amidst the ruins of her past, a flicker of hope remained. The future, though uncertain, held a glimmer of possibility. The world was still a fragile place, full of hope and despair. But as Delia walked into the unknown, she carried within her the knowledge that she had made a difference, that her actions had shifted the course of history, even if the cost had been immeasurable.

She would continue on, her heart heavy with the weight of her past, but her spirit unbroken. The price of freedom was a burden she would carry, but it would also lead her on a new quest. The betrayal of the director, Elena and Thorne gave her pause and she understood that the evil they were a part of still thrived in this new world. She would do what needed to be done to ensure that the evil never had a chance to flourish.

| 42 |

Delia's Revival

The trees pressed in, a suffocating blanket of damp earth and decaying leaves. Each rustle, each snap of a twig was amplified in the oppressive darkness, a counterpoint to the rhythmic *thump-thump-thump* of her own heart. Delia saw them—the shadows, the surveillance teams, patient predators, their eyes burning holes in the night, waiting for her to slip up.

Slithering from the trees, she moved like a wraith, a whisper of movement against the dark night. She reached the back door to the garage, unlocking it, hoping that each click of the tumbler was not a betrayal of the silence she craved. The alarm panel was dark. She let out a quiet laugh. David, bless his trusting, uncomplicated heart, would never remember. He'd been raised on open fields and honest hands; the notion of security systems was as foreign as a locked door. It was his naivete, his unwavering faith, that she loved.

She slipped off her boots and stepped onto the cold tile floor. The immaculate kitchen made her chuckle. Not a dish out of place. David's obsessive orderliness was a stark contrast to the chaos she carried within. The memories of the cookies, the pies, his simple joys, haunted the air, a painful reminder of what she might lose.

He'd never questioned her absences. High-powered attorney, international clients, secrets she couldn't share— it was the perfect cover for her double life. She had called him twice and left messages that she was fine, that the negotiations for her client were going well and that she hoped to be home in a few days. His trust was unwavering.

Saving Thorne from himself had become a self-inflicted wound, a festering infection. The scent of his life—his home—was as suffocating as the jasmine perfume worn by Elena, a potent mixture almost too much to bear. It had threatened to break her. But she never gave up on David. She had no idea why he had lied to her, but she no longer cared. She lied to him all the time. Fair was fair. David was the best part of her life, and someday they would be together without all the secrets. She had to believe that.

She climbed the stairs, each step a measured beat against the silence. She pushed open the bedroom door. There he was. David. Sound asleep, his soft snores a painful counterpoint to the storm in her soul. His peaceful face was so vulnerable, so utterly trusting. And the knowledge of her betrayal was an icy fist clenching around her heart.

Delia stripped off her clothes at the end of the bed and slid her pistol under the mattress. In the moonlight, she checked to make sure her bandages were still in place. Silent as a breeze, she slipped under the covers and pressed her body against his back. She could feel the fire burn between her legs as she longed for his touch. She reached under the covers and ran her fingers along his body, stopping as she felt his urge grow. He reached for the light.

"Leave the light off," she said.

He turned and faced her, his hands moving over her body. He stopped at the bandage on her side.

"You're injured," he said, his eyes seeking an answer.

She took his hand and placed it on her breast. "It's nothing to worry about," she whispered.

His fingers worked their magic, and soon they were tangled in each other, holding on to each other through the throes of passion. Delia, reaching her climax at the same time he did, screamed into the pillow, her body shaking, her skin crawling. She fell back onto the bed and snuggled into his shoulder.

David leaned on one elbow and looked into her eyes. He never noticed the red hair that had replaced her golden locks.

"Are you home for good?" he asked.

She smiled at him, soaking in his smells. "I have one more thing to take care of, and then I will be home."

"Be careful," he said. He rolled onto his pillow and fell into a blissful sleep. When he woke the next morning, Delia was gone, her side of the bed a jumble of sheets and a memory that he would hold on to.

Delia had slipped out during the night. Her leaving hurt, but what she had to do was more important than anything she had done before. She headed for the private executive airport and a flight from which she might not return.

| 43 |

The Aftermath

The air hummed with an energy that only New York City could provide. It was a stark contrast to the easy-going life of her home in California. It had been years since she had been here, but the city remained little changed. The world had averted a catastrophe, but the scars remained. The city, a vibrant hub of commerce and innovation, now carried the weight of a collective sigh of relief, tinged with a lingering fear. Life was returning to its familiar rhythm, yet the world had shifted on its axis, and the aftershocks were still being felt.

Delia sat on the hotel room balcony, her morning coffee still steaming in the cup in her hands. The familiar scent of freshly brewed coffee, a comforting ritual, was now a reminder of the normalcy she had almost lost. Her gaze drifted to the street, where people headed to work or shopping or wherever, unaware of the shadow of danger they had dodged. The fragile world was like a delicate butterfly wing that a single wrong move could shatter.

The events of the past week were etched into her memory, every detail a sharp, jagged piece of a mosaic she couldn't erase: the betrayal, the chase, the agonizing decisions she had made. The world had demanded a price, which she had willingly paid.

The world was a different place now, and she was different too. The world had seen a different version of her, the one who wasn't afraid to fight, who was willing to sacrifice everything for what she believed in. She had shown the world her true self, the one who could wield death as a weapon, but also the one who could love with an intensity that bordered on recklessness.

The world was watching, waiting to see how she would pick up the pieces of her life. She was a warrior, a survivor who had walked on the edge of darkness and emerged with her soul intact but forever changed. She had saved the world, a choice that had cost her dearly.

Now the world was breathing again, but she was still struggling to catch her breath. She wasn't sure what the future held, but she knew one thing for certain: her life would never be the same. The past week had shattered the illusion of normalcy she had cultivated. She had faced her demons, confronted her past and emerged with a renewed sense of purpose.

Delia finished her coffee and walked into her room. After a quick shower and a change of bandages, she slipped into her business suit: a pale blue jacket and skirt, the skirt stopping six inches above her knees, black high heels that accentuated her legs and a thin white blouse that barely contained her. The outfit left nothing to the imagination.

She strapped the two composite knives onto her thighs and checked herself in the mirror. She looked incredible. Very businesslike, and sexy as hell. The red hair accented the final picture. She was ready; she grabbed her black shoulder bag and headed for the lobby.

The car she had ordered was waiting, and she tipped the doorman and slid inside. The driver, silent through the drive, pulled up in front of the Suliman Industries high-rise in Manhattan, and Delia slid out of the car. The driver would wait for her.

Delia followed the secretary as she knocked on the large oak door and pushed it open.

"Ms. Delia Cahill, sir," said the secretary as she stepped aside and let Delia pass. She closed the door.

Benjamin Suliman rose from behind his desk, walked around and, after taking a quick glimpse at Delia, reached out his hand.

"Benjamin Suliman. Pleased to meet you." They shook hands. He pointed towards one of the two leather chairs in front of the desk, and Delia sat down, letting her skirt slide up her thigh a little more. She set her shoulder bag on the floor next to the chair.

Benjamin Suliman was over six feet tall and was just a tad overweight for his height. He carried himself well, and Delia could understand why the billionaire industrialist was so widely respected. His silver hair and medium complexion gave him a look of authority. Suliman also carried a secret. He bankrolled the largest terrorist organization in the world.

Suliman offered coffee or something stronger from the small bar behind his desk, but Delia refused. He poured himself a coffee and sat behind the desk, Delia catching the way his eyes followed her legs.

"So, Ms. Cahill. Your clientele list is very impressive, but one thing I have more than enough of is attorneys, so what can I do for you this fine morning?"

Suliman spoke with a hint of a Middle Eastern accent with just a touch of British. She leaned back in her chair, which caused her blouse to open a little further, enticing his eyes.

"Mr. Suliman, I'll get right to the point. I have something you want. Something you were willing to pay a tremendous amount of money for, and I'd like to sell it to you."

Suliman stared at her for a moment, his mind working.

"I have no idea what you are talking about." He stared at the red hair, and she wondered if he found it familiar.

Delia smiled. "This something was supposed to be provided to you by an individual who is now deceased, and the woman representing your interest has since vanished without a trace."

Suliman gave nothing away as he watched her. He knew she had no weapons or electronic devices, since she had passed through the hidden screener as she entered his office.

"This item," she said, "has come into my possession, and I really have no need for it. I do not know for certain what your final offer was, but I know that the original seller had requested an increase in the price at the last minute. Since my needs are significantly less than your first representative,

I would be willing to offer it to you for half of your original offer. Quite the deal, Mr. Suliman."

She uncrossed her legs and recrossed them, her skirt riding higher up her thigh. Suliman didn't hide his stare. He tented his fingers and leaned back in his chair.

"How do I know that you have this item?" he asked, never taking his eyes off her legs.

Delia smiled. "Unlike your previous representative, I work with my clients from a basis of trust. You can ask any of them, and they will tell you the same thing. If we can come to an agreement, I will provide you with the item. You can have your experts validate its authenticity, and then you will deposit the agreed-upon amount into an account I provide you. Simple and clean."

"And is there a deadline connected to this item?"

"No, sir. No threats. No deadline. I am giving you the first right of refusal, but an agreement will need to be reached before I leave. If at the end of this conversation you choose not to purchase the item, we will shake hands and forget we have ever met. If you decide to accept the offer, then you tell me how long you need to make the arrangements."

Suliman looked her up and down. He had never dealt with a woman of such confidence, someone who had not wilted in his presence.

"I will accept your offer, Ms. Cahill. I will have someone reach out to you to accept the item for validation. Your terms are most acceptable, and it is refreshing doing business with a professional."

Delia stood and reached across the desk, her blouse giving Suliman a generous view. They shook hands.

"Now, about that drink," she said. She stepped around the desk and walked towards the bar. "Allow me," she said.

As she walked past his chair, her thigh brushed against his hand on the armrest, and he opened his fingers and slid them along her thigh. She stepped behind his chair and poured two drinks. As she did, she slid her hand under her skirt and removed one of her knives.

She turned and leaned around the chair to set his drink in front of him, and he nonchalantly reached up and touched her breast.

The knife slid into the side of his neck and she raked it across his throat, slicing through his vocal cords. He grabbed his throat as she stepped aside to avoid the arterial spray. He struggled for breath and voice. Neither one came. His head slumped to the side, and his breathing ceased. Delia finished her drink and washed the knife and her hands in the bar sink.

She plugged a USB drive into the side of his laptop, waited for the password to be bypassed and opened his banking application. She transferred 2.5 billion dollars, the agreed-upon amount, to a secret account that instantly transferred the money into numerous other accounts around the world, and the amount disappeared from his screen. She closed his laptop, pulled the USB and picked up her bag. She walked to the door, turned and looked at Suliman.

"It was a pleasure doing business with you, Mr. Suliman," she said with a smile.

She opened the door and stepped out, closing it behind her. She stepped up to the secretary's desk.

"Mr. Suliman asked me to let you know he will be reviewing our contract and does not want to be disturbed. Thank you."

She exited the building, slid into the waiting car and was at the executive airport and in the air within thirty minutes of leaving Suliman's office. She sat back in the seat and sipped her champagne.

| 44 |

The Path Forward

Delia leaned against the railing of the balcony, watching the sun dip below the horizon, painting the sky in hues of orange and crimson. The resort, far from her California home, had been a refuge and place of relaxation for years. It was also a place where she was anonymous.

The events of the past few weeks—the relentless chase, the agonizing choices, the heart-wrenching sacrifices— had left an indelible mark on her soul. It was as if she had been through a thousand lifetimes in the blink of an eye. She was a woman transformed, her worldview irrevocably altered.

The world she knew, the world of shadows and secrets, was now a distant memory. She had shed the skin of the assassin, the cold-blooded killer who operated in the realm of darkness, and emerged into a fragile, uncertain light. Yet a part of her remained trapped in that world, haunted by the echoes of her past.

The whispers of the Organization still lingered in her ears, like a phantom that refused to be silenced. She had defied their orders, challenged their authority, and in doing so, she had shattered the foundation of her existence. The price she had paid, the weight of her choices, was heavy on her heart. But there was also a newfound sense of freedom, a liberation that came with defying the shackles of her former life.

She had glimpsed the possibility of a different path, a life where she could choose her own destiny, where love and compassion could coexist with the darkness within her.

The billionaire, the enigmatic recluse she had chosen to protect, had shown her a world beyond the limitations she had imposed on herself. He had challenged her perceptions, forced her to confront her own humanity. But her future remained uncertain. The threat she had faced, the looming catastrophe that she had averted, still cast a long shadow over her life. She was not free from danger. Her enemies were still out there, lurking in the shadows, waiting for an opportunity to strike.

Delia knew she could not walk away from her past. The Organization, the life she had lived, would never let her go. They would always be a part of her, woven into the fabric of her being. But she also knew that she could not remain trapped in the darkness. She had to reconcile her past with her present, to build a future that embraced the light and acknowledged the shadows.

The thought of David, his warm smile, his gentle touch, offered a flicker of hope amid her turmoil. Their connection, forged in the crucible of danger and sacrifice, was as strong as it was fragile. But Delia knew she had to be cautious, that her heart was a dangerous thing, capable of leading her down a path of destruction.

She needed time, time to heal, time to find herself. Time to decide who she wanted to be, what she wanted to fight for. The road ahead was uncertain, filled with both promise and peril. But Delia knew one thing for certain: she would face whatever came her way, armed with the courage of her convictions and the unwavering strength of her heart, and when she was ready, she would bring David back into her life. He never questioned her need to get away, telling her only that he was there when she needed him. She knew she could make this work.

The air grew cooler as darkness enveloped the island paradise. Delia shivered, not from the cold, but from the weight of her thoughts. She drew a deep breath, letting the salty air fill her lungs, and looked out at the distant lights of the harbor, each one a beacon of hope in the encroaching darkness. She knew she had to find her way, to create her own light in the world. She had to forge a new dawn, one that reflected the strength she had discovered within herself.

As she turned to leave the balcony, a sudden gust of wind stirred the air, carrying with it the scent of jasmine and the faint sound of distant laughter. Delia paused, listening, a faint smile gracing her lips. It was a reminder that even in the darkest of nights, life found a way to bloom. And she too would bloom, even if it was amidst the ruins of her past.

| 45 |

The New Beginning

Retired United States Senator Calvin March sat in the chair in the gentleman's club and sipped his bourbon. He occupied the same seat that his predecessor had while he was the director of the Organization. Across from him sat his guest, drinking his beer from a crystal glass instead of the bottle.

"Do we know where she is?" asked March.

"No, sir, but we have all our resources looking for her. We'll find her," said the guest.

"It's been, what, almost six months since Thorne died? How can she still be hidden?"

The guest smiled. "We trained her. She's one of the best we ever had. She could be sitting in this room right now and we wouldn't know it. She's that good."

"Do you think someone is helping her?" asked March.

The guest sipped his beer. "We've reached out to anyone she ever knew or worked with. No one has heard from her. Delia is more than capable of disappearing on her own."

The new director took a sip of his drink. "She caused a lot of damage in her betrayal," said March.

The guest chuckled, and March looked at him.

"What?" he asked.

"Delia wasn't the only one who betrayed us," said the guest. "Your predecessor betrayed us all, and he paid the ultimate price. It has recently come to our attention that he was working with a woman who was once part of our team but who died almost twenty years ago, killed by Delia. It seems she didn't die, and she helped corrupt the last director."

The director frowned. "The end does not justify the means."

"No, sir," said the guest, "but it adds a little clarity, and maybe in the end Delia had her reasons for betraying us. Maybe we lost focus on our mission, the way she did on hers. We may never know."

"Where is the FBI with the Suliman investigation?" asked the director.

"They now know that Suliman was the intended buyer of Thorne's program. They have identified many of the dead from the beach house as members of various terrorist cells that he was financing."

"Did Delia kill him?" asked March.

"It looks like she did. They have a security video from the building showing a redhead entering and leaving around the time of his death. He also had a meeting on the books with Delia Cahill, attorney. He met with the redhead just prior to his death. We believe it was Delia sporting a new look."

"It seems we have a lot to uncover yet," March said, his eyes narrowing. "Delia Cahill, an enigma. It's intriguing, to say the least." He took another sip of his bourbon, his eyes never leaving those of his guest.

"Tell me about Delia Cahill," said March. "How did she become so skilled at evading capture?"

"Delia was always a talented operative, but her true specialty was infiltration and deception. She could become anyone she wanted, change her appearance and mannerisms to suit the mission. It's why she was so effective, and why she's so hard to find now."

March stroked his chin, deep in thought. "A chameleon, of sorts. Adaptable, elusive. It seems we underestimated her. But why would she turn against us? What could have driven her to such extremes?"

The guest shook his head, a hint of sadness in his eyes. "That, we may never know. Delia kept her motives close to her chest. But one thing is certain: she planned this meticulously. Her disappearance was no accident."

March's gaze hardened. "We must find her, then. Uncover her motives and bring her to justice. Too much is at stake."

"Indeed, sir," the guest replied. "Our agents are following every lead, no matter how small. We will find Delia Cahill, and when we do, we will get the answers we seek."

March nodded, his expression grim. "See that you do," he said. "The fate of the Organization may depend on it."

As the guest rose to leave, March added, "And remember, we must also uncover the truth behind the late director's betrayal. There are still shadows lurking in the Organization, and we must shine a light on them."

David Cahill stood, shook the director's hand and walked out of the room. He smiled as he left.

ACKNOWLEDGMENTS

A special thank you to my daughter Christina J. Morgan, my unofficial collaborator.

Thanks to my editor, Laura Dragonette, whose efforts helped turn my manuscript into a polished novel. Her help is greatly appreciated. Any mistakes the reader may find are solely the responsibility of the author.

Also, I would like to thank my family for their encouragement. I have been telling them stories since they were little, and I always told them that someone should be writing this stuff down. I decided to write it down myself.

A special thanks to my late wife, Jane. She pushed me for years to become a writer, and my biggest regret is that she didn't live long enough to see it happen. I love her with all my heart and miss her every day. I think she would be pleased.

Finally, thanks to the readers. Without you, none of this would be important.

ABOUT THE AUTHOR

1. Pacific Book Awards Best Mystery Finalist . . . *Crime Delayed*
2. Pacific Book Awards Best Mystery Winner . . . *Crime Denied*
3. Chanticleer International Book Awards: 1st

Place Blue Ribbon, CLUE Book Awards for Suspense, Thriller Fiction . . . *Crime Denied*

1. Chanticleer International Book Awards Finalist, CLUE Book Awards for Suspense, Thriller Fiction . . . *Crime Conspiracy*
2. Chanticleer International Book Awards Finalist,

Book Series, CLUE Book Awards for Suspense, Thriller Fiction . . . Crime Series, The Buck Taylor Novels

1. Chanticleer International Book Awards Finalist, CLUE Book Awards for Suspense, Thriller Fiction . . . *Crime Exploded*

2. **Chanticleer International Book Awards Finalist, CLUE Book Awards for Suspense, Thriller Fiction ...** *Crime Spree*
3. **Chanticleer International Book Awards Finalist, CLUE Book Awards for Suspense, Thriller Fiction ...**

Crime Scene

2023 Chanticleer International Book Awards Series Finalist, Mystery & Mayhem Book Awards ... *Crime Series.*

Chuck Morgan attended Seton Hall University and Regis College and spent thirty-five years as a construction project manager. He is an avid outdoorsman, an Eagle Scout and a licensed private pilot. He enjoys camping, hiking, mountain biking and fly-fishing.

He is the author of the Crime series, featuring Colorado Bureau of Investigation Agent Buck Taylor. The series includes *Crime Interrupted, Crime Delayed, Crime Unsolved, Crime Exposed, Crime Denied, Crime Conspiracy, Crime Unknown, Crime Exploded, Crime Spree, Crime Scene and Crime Victims.*

He is also the author of *Her Name Was Jane*, a memoir about his late wife's nine-year battle with breast cancer. He has three children, and four grandchildren. He resides in Lone Tree, Colorado.

OTHER BOOKS BY THE AUTHOR

Dear Reader, thank you for reading this novel. Please enjoy the other books in this series and follow Colorado Bureau of Investigator Buck Taylor and his team as they investigate new and sometimes unusual crimes in the Colorado mountains. Each novel is a separate story, and they can be read in any order, but you might find it more enjoyable to read them in order. Happy Reading

Chuck Morgan

"Crime Interrupted: A Buck Taylor Novel by Chuck Morgan is a gripping, edge-of-the-seat novel. *Right from page one,*

the action kicks off and never stops, gaining pace as each chapter passes." Reviewed by Anne-Marie Reynolds for Readers' Favorite.

Finalist . . . 2019 Pacific Book Awards Best Mystery

"**This crime novel reads like a great thriller.** *The writing is atmospheric, laced with vivid descriptions that capture the setting in great detail while allowing readers to follow the intensity of the action and the emotional and psychological depth of the story.*" *Reviewed by Divine Zape for Readers' Favorite.*

"*Professionally written in the style of a best-selling crime novelist, such as Tom Clancy, Crime Unsolved: A Buck Taylor Novel by Chuck Morgan is a spellbinding suspense novel with*

an environmental flair. Intriguing subplots of fraud, sur-vivalist paranoia and murder weave their way through the fab-ric of the plot, creating a dynamic story. This is an action-filled, stimulating tale which contains fascinating details that are rele-vant in our present climate." Reviewed by Susan Sewell for Read-ers' Favorite.

CHUCK MORGAN

CRIME
EXPOSED

A BUCK TAYLOR NOVEL

"Chuck Morgan has a unique gift for plot, one that makes
Crime Exposed: A Buck Taylor Novel a hard-to-put-down book.
From the start, readers know what happens to Barb, but they be-

come curious as they follow the investigation, wondering if the characters will find out what happened to her. The descriptions are filled with clarity, and they offer readers great images. The prose is elegant, and it captures both the emotional and psychological elements of the novel clearly while offering vivid descriptions of scenes and characters. This is a fast-paced thriller with memorable characters and a criminal investigation that is so real readers will believe it could happen." Reviewed by Romuald Dzemo for Readers' Favorite.

Winner ... 2020 Pacific Book Awards Best Mystery

1. **Chanticleer International Book Awards: 1st Place Blue Ribbon, CLUE Book Awards for Suspense, Thriller Fiction**

"It's really progressive to see a female serial killer portrayed with such intelligent writing and depth of character, *and the cat and mouse chase dynamic is thrown off nicely by the* *switching of genders. What results is a really enjoyable thriller* *and crime mystery novel, and overall Crime Denied is certain to* *please fans of both hard-boiled detective tales and action/adventure crime novels."* Reviewed by K.C. Finn for Readers' Favorite.

1. Chanticleer International Book Awards Finalist, CLUE Book Awards for Suspense, Thriller Fiction ... *Crime Conspiracy*

"This makes for a truly dynamic story where anything is possible, and a hero you can root for even when it looks like all is lost." Reviewed by K.C. Finn for Readers' Favorite.

"This is a book you can't put down, which will entertain you on many levels, and at times make your skin crawl; the kind of book that remains in your thoughts long after you finish reading." Reviewed by Steven Robson for Readers' Favorite.

AWARD WINNING AUTHOR
CHUCK MORGAN

CRIME
UNKNOWN

A BUCK TAYLOR NOVEL

"I read Crime Unknown in one sitting. The plot is intense and the main character agent Buck Taylor is a hero like no other. This book has everything a thriller needs to be and more. I thought I knew the story at the beginning. Buck will solve a tricky murder case, I thought. But Chuck Morgan adds a twist to this story that expands it and makes it one of the most enjoyable books I've read in this genre. I loved that the lead was such an awesome well-rounded fellow but that he also had a support team who were just as important to the story."* Reviewed by Maureen Dangarembizi for Readers' Favorite.

"Crime Unknown is a thoroughly enjoyable read and I would not hesitate to recommend this book to fans of the crime genre and those looking for a gateway in." Reviewed by K.C. Finn for Readers' Favorite.

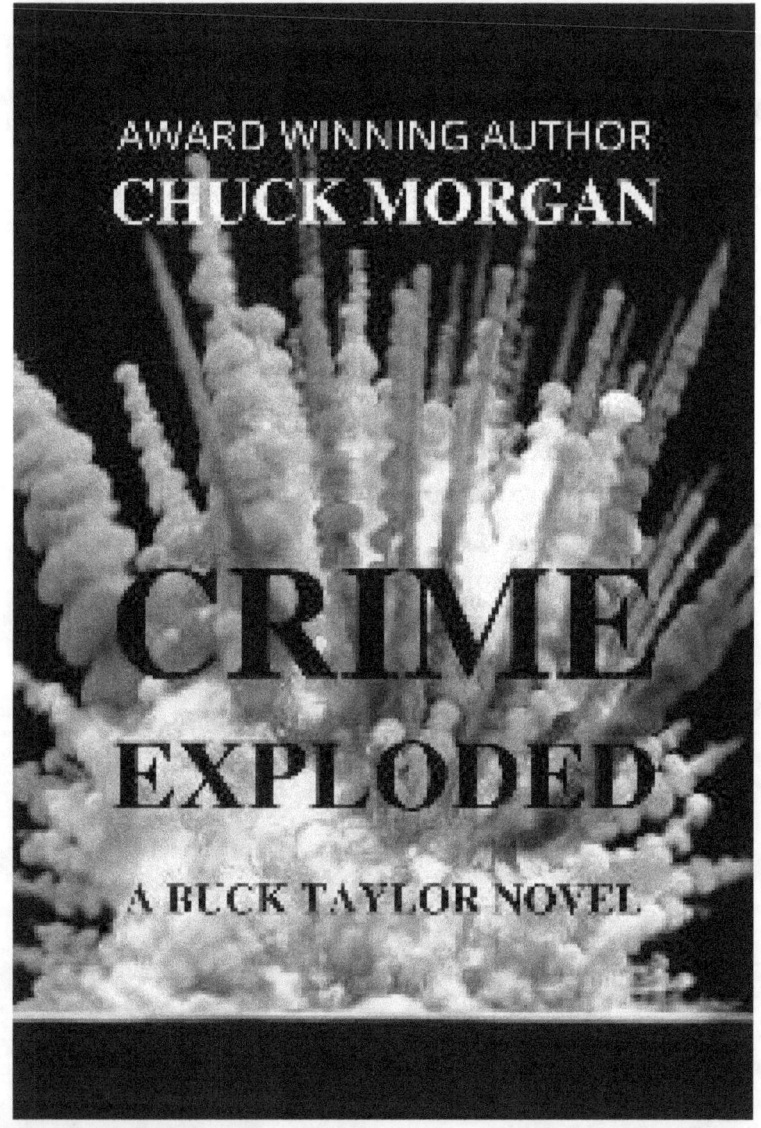

2022 Chanticleer International Book Awards Finalist, CLUE Book Awards for Suspense, Thriller Fiction . . . *Crime Exploded*

"Action-packed and fast-paced, I was sucked into the story the moment I opened the novel. The author built the story to perfection. Chuck Morgan gave just the right amount of suspense, mystery, and action to keep readers' attention on Buck and his team. There was never a dull moment in the story. The narrative ran smoothly until the end; it followed the development of the story and the pace set by the characters. I enjoyed the twists and turns. What I loved more than anything else in the plot was how calculating Buck was. He was smart; he didn't let the FBI discourage him and kept his head in the game. The action gave me an adrenaline rush. Absolutely brilliant!" Rabia Tanveer for Readers' Favorite.

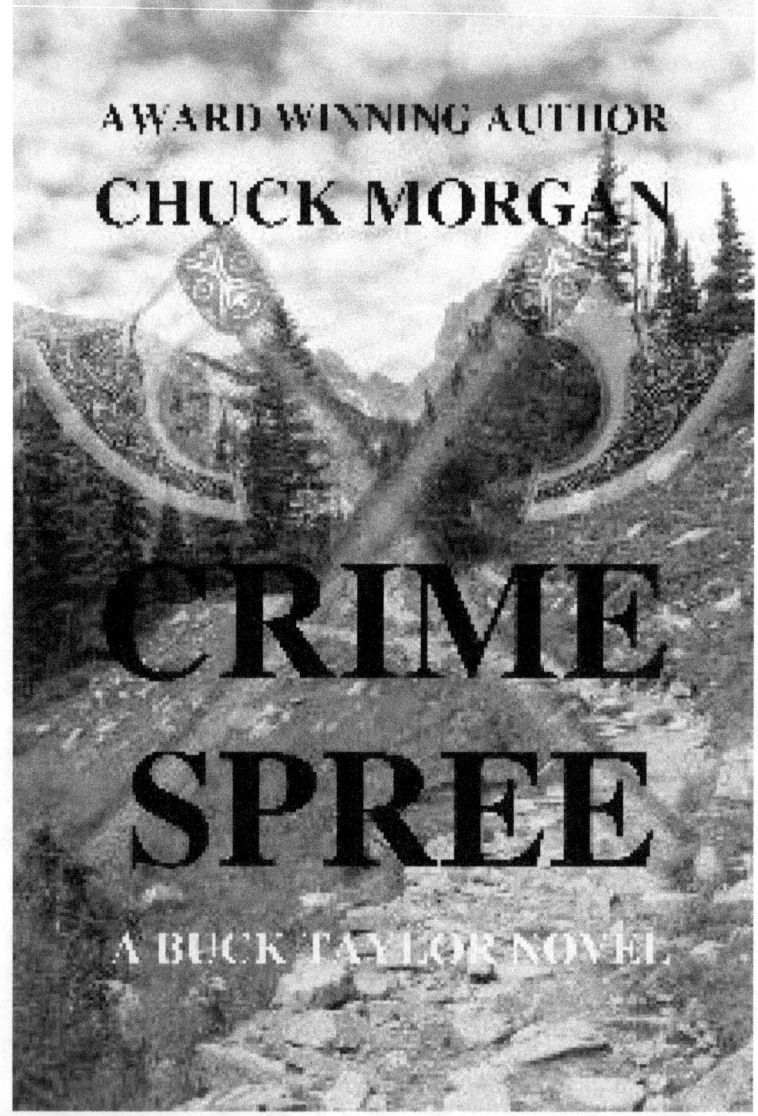

2022 Chanticleer International Book Awards Finalist, CLUE Book Awards for Suspense, Thriller Fiction . . . *Crime Spree*

"*It is one of the best crime novels I have read in a long while, with real characters developed in a way to let you get to know them intimately, understand them, and appreciate their strengths and weaknesses.* The plot is tight, exciting, and tense, with plenty of action, and it will grip you from the start. The bizarre storyline is enthralling, written in descriptive prose that lands you right in the middle of the action. Forget sleep; once you pick this book up, you won't want to put it down until it's finished. Fantastic story, and highly recommended for fans of high-octane crime thrillers.*" Reviewed by Anne-Marie Reynolds for Readers' Favorite.

*"**Crime Family is the tenth book in the Buck Taylor series. Chuck Morgan had me hooked from the first page until the end.** There was never a dull moment with all the action; one chapter flowed into the next. The story was fast-paced and kept me on the edge of my seat. I kept turning the pages to find out what would happen next. I was intrigued, and with all the twists and turns, I could not predict what was looming. The characters were well-developed. Each had a background description, and it was fun getting to know some of them. The story was excellently written with a fitting ending." Reviewed by Alma Boucher for Readers' Favorite.*

"Crime Scene is a must-read for lovers of mystery sleuth and murder tales with a touch of conspiracy." Reader's Favorite review.

"*Crime Scene has a carefully designed intrigue that deepens with every unforeseeable turn of events and a dynamic narrative.*" *Reader's Favorite review.*

"*This is a great book. Holds your attention and you don't want to put down. I would recommend this book to anyone who loves a good crime novel.*" *Amazon review.*

"*Spellbinding, gripping, powerful, and relevant are just a few words that come to mind after turning the last page of "Crime Scene: A Buck Taylor Novel, book 11, by Chuck Morgan.*" *Amazon Review.*

AWARD-WINNING AUTHOR
CHUCK MORGAN

CRIME VICTIMS

A BUCK TAYLOR NOVEL

"*A riveting plot and good pacing keep the reader in suspense as Buck Taylor and his team establish evidence beyond a reasonable doubt.* The author sustains interest by skillfully showing the art and intuition involved in crime investigation and the science behind it, as well as the elements that can delay or confound it. There are a lot of quirky characters in the novel and the author gives them mannerisms, voices, and descriptions that make them distinctive and realistic. The details and descriptions of the work and everyday life of the players are both pleasantly appealing and revolting, depending on the scenario. What's most captivating and intriguing about the character development is the backstory of the unhinged characters and how the author uses them as part of the perplexing trail of a horrendous crime. Themes of sadism, cruelty, grief, forensics, police procedures, and even a little bit of romance can be found in this installment of the Buck Taylor series. Highly recommended for crime story fans who especially enjoy the information as well as the twists, turns, and the untangling of intricate and cold case crime sprees." Reviewed by Carmen Tenorio for Readers' Favorite.

Resurrection by Chuck Morgan presents a riveting, suspense-filled story involving the Nazis and a plan to gain power in modern-day New York. It's 2024, and the Nazis are back with vengeance. Reader's Favorite Review

If you're a fan of thrillers and history, get this book today! . Reader's Favorite Review

Chuck Morgan has penned a unique, fascinating story with sharp, believable dialogue that perfectly drives the plot forward. The pacing is impressive and immersive. . Reader's Favorite Review

This is a literary masterpiece that would make an intriguing movie. Bravo to Mr. Morgan for writing a story examining the "what if" element that reflects on the impact of history in today's world. . Reader's Favorite Review